THE REASON FOR JANEY

By the same author
Bringing Nettie Back

THE
REASON FOR
JANEY

Nancy Hope Wilson

Macmillan Publishing Company
New York

Maxwell Macmillan Canada
Toronto

Maxwell Macmillan International
New York   Oxford   Singapore   Sydney

Macmillan Publishing Company is part of the Maxwell Communication
Group of Companies. Macmillan Publishing Company, 866 Third Avenue, New York,
NY 10022. Maxwell Macmillan Canada, Inc., 1200 Eglinton Avenue East, Suite 200,
Don Mills, Ontario M3C 3N1
First edition. Printed in the United States of America

10 9 8 7 6 5 4 3 2 1

The text of this book is set in 12 point Berkeley Oldstyle Book.

Permission to reprint two lines of "Poem for a Lady Whose Voice I Like," from *The
Women and the Men* by Nikki Giovanni, copyright © 1975 by Nikki Giovanni, is
gratefully acknowledged to William Morrow & Company, Inc.

Library of Congress Cataloging-in-Publication Data
Wilson, Nancy Hope.
The reason for Janey / by Nancy Hope Wilson.
— 1st ed.
p.   cm.
Summary: Philly's life changes greatly when, after her parents' divorce, her mother
takes in Janey, a retarded adult, to live with them.
ISBN 0-02-793127-7
[1. Mentally handicapped—Fiction. 2. Interpersonal relations—Fiction. 3.
Divorce—Fiction. 4. Family life—Fiction.]   I. Title.
PZ7.W69745Re   1994
[Fic]—dc20   93-22930

To Nick, Hannah, and Caleb:
the three main reasons for my happiness

ACKNOWLEDGMENTS

Both this book and my life have been greatly enriched by my friends Jane Curlin and Theresa Pelletrino. As I presumed to help them learn about fastening seat belts or making coffee, they taught me far more important lessons about the strength of the human spirit.

For ideas and resources on science curriculum, I am grateful to Wanita Laffond and her 1990–1991 sixth graders at the Buckland-Shelburne Regional Elementary School.

Immeasurable thanks to my critique group for their patience and wisdom as I sorted out the tangles in this story, and especially to Cynthia Stowe, Jessie Haas, and Michael Daley for their generous attention to the complete manuscript. Thanks, as well, to Judith R. Whipple, whose suggestions seem always to empower me.

and he said: you pretty full of yourself ain't chu
so she replied: show me someone not full of herself
and i'll show you a hungry person

Nikki Giovanni

I don't get it. The reason for Janey, I mean.

I like to know the reasons for things. When I know the reason for something, it fits. I can manage it. For the fifth-grade science fair last year, I worked on the reason for rain. I spent so much time in the library, my best friend, April, got mad at me, but I wanted to know the reason—I mean, really understand why there's rain. I'm just like that.

I made rain, too. Right there in booth number fifteen in the gym. It won me first prize. Danny Stapleton still can't get over it. I guess coming in only second was a first for Danny.

I sure didn't mind getting that blue ribbon, but the best part was knowing the reason for rain.

It's harder figuring out the reason for Janey. I usually go to the library after school, and last May, when Janey first came, I read a lot about mental retardation. Maybe when Janey was born, she didn't get enough oxygen. Or maybe when she was a kid, there was lead in the water pipes. There could be plenty of reasons why it's hard for Janey to learn things.

But those reasons don't explain why she fits. I mean, in our family and all.

The guy from Home Care kept warning my kid brother and me it would be a big change when Janey moved in. He sounded like the school counselor who talked to us three years ago, when Dad moved out: "Big change."

"Difficult adjustments." But Dad had started leaving before he left. I mean, he could leave when he was still right there in the room, arguing with Mom. If it weren't for Boomer and me going to visit once a month, I bet Dad would keep right on leaving, till he'd forget to notice he ever had two kids. Dad weekends may not be a carnival, but they aren't a "difficult adjustment," either. They just keep my father being my father.

The truth is, the only "big change" I remember from the divorce was things getting peaceful all of a sudden.

But I figured having a retarded person in the family would take some getting used to. That's the trouble. That's what I don't understand. Janey just fits. It took Boomer maybe two days to get Janey playing Parcheesi with him (which I was sick of doing). And it didn't take me much longer to realize that even though Janey's a grown-up, she acts more like a friend. There's got to be a reason why somebody I never knew till four months ago fits into my family better than Dad *ever* did.

I've tried asking Mom about the reason for Janey, but Mom just explains all over again how Janey has no family, so of course we welcome her in ours. Or she goes on about the money Home Care pays—for room and board, and for teaching Janey things.

Mom's just not big on reasons. The only excuse she's got for Boomer's and my names is that her great-grandparents were Boomer and Philura Higley. But why should someone else have decided who I have to be?

I mean, if I'm stuck being Philura Higley Mason, at least I ought to have a good reason.

SEPTEMBER

1

I'd just gotten home and grabbed an orange from the fridge when Janey came in the front door.

"Hi," I said. "How're you doing?"

"Hi, Philly," she said, smiling like I was something special. "I'm home now, Philly." Janey's two front teeth stick out a little, but it's her eyes you notice when she smiles. They're so dark, and set so deep in her face, she seems to be looking out from somewhere far away. But her smile makes them sparkle and kind of leap with light. "How are you, Philly?" she asked.

"Okay," I said. "How about you?"

"I'm fine, Philly."

She kept smiling and set down her short-handled red pocketbook to take off her jacket. Janey's really pale, and so far she still wears the clothes she brought from Morrisville—pull-on pink polyester pants and pastel blue overblouses. They make her look all soft and lumpy. I keep telling Mom we ought to get Janey some jeans, but Mom says that's up to Janey. "Suppose I decided you ought to wear dresses," Mom says, and I get her point.

Using both hands, Janey hung the jacket carefully on a coat hook. Then she opened the pocketbook and took out her mismatched pack of playing cards. She transferred them to her pocket and smiled some more. She always keeps those cards with her, but I wonder about the reason, because when Boomer and I tried to teach her some card games, she wasn't interested.

"How was work?" I asked. I meant her day program, where they're going to teach her a job.

Janey's mouth still smiled, but her eyes looked away, and she held totally still for a second. Her arms froze, crooked, out in front of her, so she looked like a marionette whose strings had gotten stuck. When she thought of what to say, everything jerked and came unstuck.

"Good, Philly." Her eyes gleamed at me again. "I like work. I do!"

I tossed my orange up and caught it. "Your hair's getting longer," I said. Janey's hair is dark like mine, but straight, and when she first came here four months ago, it was chopped so short and ragged, she looked like a kid whose big sister'd just cut her hair with the pinking shears. I know, because my Aunt Nolly did that to Mom when they were little, and Mom still has a picture.

Janey touched her hair with her palm. "It's getting longer, Philly," she said. "Polly says so, too."

"What about me?" Mom asked, bursting in from her studio. She headed for the kitchen, making sort of a breeze as she passed. Her hair was falling down in wisps around her face, and her long skirt fluttered. "Hi, Janey. Good day? Hi, Curly Top. Where's April? Oh, yeah. Thursday. Gymnastics."

I started peeling my orange as I followed Mom into the kitchen and sat down at the table.

Janey paused in the hall, saying, "I'm fine, Polly. How are you?" Then she came and stood in the doorway, fingering that little-girl locket of hers—a gold heart strung with pink and white beads. I guess Janey doesn't have much jewelry. "How are you, Polly?" she said.

Mom was squatting in front of a cabinet, rummaging around among the cans. She had on a white blouse, but there was black ink on the elbows. "Fine, Janey," she said, "but awful busy." The thing about doing graphic design freelance like Mom does is that sometimes she doesn't have enough work, and sometimes she has too much. "It's like this every September," she muttered. She stood up and plunked a couple of cans of Chickarina soup in front of me. "Could you two make supper? There's some French bread in the freezer, I think. Tell Boomer it's his turn to clean up. And Janey, could you make a salad?"

"Sure, Polly! I like making salads." Janey went straight to the fridge and started pulling out the lettuce and cucumber.

"Great," Mom said. "All set, Curly Top?" She smiled at me and ruffled my hair.

"No problem," I said through a mouthful of orange, but Mom had already headed for her studio again. She'd eat rice cakes, and maybe a yogurt, later.

Of all the things Janey's learned so far, making salads is her favorite. It takes her a long time, but I had to thaw the bread anyway. She peeled the cucumber strip by strip and cut it very carefully, laying the slices on top of the lettuce like eggs in a nest. When the soup and bread were hot, and Boomer had shown up to eat, Janey took the salad bowl in both hands and placed it in the middle of the table like a chef's prize dish. She smiled around at Boomer and me.

Boomer didn't notice. He was making a couple of peanut-butter-and-ketchup sandwiches to have instead of the French bread. He was wearing his little tape player and had the headset on, so his hair stuck up funny all around the band. Boomer actually listens to Mozart and stuff. He's probably the only fourth grader in the world whose all-time top hit is a clarinet quintet. But Boomer doesn't mind being a little strange. He even likes his name.

He took off the headset when he sat down—that's a rule—but then he started grumbling about supper being only soup, and about the Dad weekend coming up. His friend Walter'd invited him bowling.

"I went bowling," Janey said, smiling at Boomer. "At Morrisville, Boomer. They took us."

"Great," I said. It was the first good thing I'd heard about the state school, and Janey'd lived there all her life.

Janey was excited just thinking about bowling. "It's fun, Boomer. Your dad can go, too. With you, Boomer."

"Yeah, sure," Boomer said. He glanced and grinned at me. The thought of Dad bowling was pretty goofy.

"Dad likes *watching* sports," I explained to Janey. "On TV, I mean."

I was about to describe Dad's video collection of Boston Celtics basketball games, but Janey spoke first: "What's his name?"

We both looked at her. Boomer slurped his soup. It was a funny question till I thought about it. With us always calling him Dad, and Mom hardly mentioning him anymore—except to say, "Your father will meet you at six-fifteen," things like that—Janey'd probably never heard his name.

"David," I said. "David R. Mason."

"George G. Nicoletto," Janey said, and we were both sort of staring at her again. After a careful spoonful of soup, she swallowed and smiled at me. "That's *my* father's name, Philly. George G. Nicoletto."

"I didn't know you *had* a father!" Boomer said.

I would have elbowed him for saying something so dumb—Boomer's not naive; he knows that, in order to get here, everybody's got to have a father—but I was busy being surprised that Janey had a last name. I supposed I must've seen it on Home Care forms, but we all just call her Janey.

"I have a father, Boomer. I do," Janey was saying. "Look." She took off her five-and-dime locket. "Here he is, Boomer." The gold heart opened on a little hinge. Janey held it out. "George G. Nicoletto."

There was also a picture of a woman.

"That looks like you," Boomer said.

Janey turned the locket and looked at it closely. She froze for a second, her arms poised in front of her. Then she jerked and spoke.

"That's my mother, Boomer. My mother died. When I was little. That's what they told me, Boomer. She died a long time ago."

17

I put out my hand, gentlelike, so Janey wouldn't have to notice if she didn't want to, but she handed the locket across to me right away.

"So where's your father *live*?" Boomer asked.

I should have stopped him then. He knows Janey doesn't have a family—that's the whole reason for Home Care. But I was studying the pictures. The woman looked like Janey, except really proud, and with long hair put up sort of like Mom's. And if that was Janey's father, it was sure an old picture, because he looked younger than Janey. He had a bushy mustache, and he was laughing.

Janey'd been thinking about Boomer's question. "Cambridge," she answered. "My father lives in Cambridge, Boomer."

I tried to signal Boomer. I mean, maybe Janey needs to believe her dad's alive. But Boomer was believing it, too. "No, that's *our* father who lives in Cambridge," he said. "Where does this George G. guy live? Florida? California?"

Janey smiled at him, looking confused.

"Where do his letters come from?" Boomer prompted.

I gave him a sharp nudge under the table. He raised his eyebrows at me to ask why.

"I think," I said, looking at him really hard, "that George G. Nicoletto moved far away—*really* far, you know, like to h-e-a-v-e-n." Janey can spell some things, but I was praying she couldn't spell that.

"Oh!" said Boomer. "Right." He shrugged at me like how was he supposed to know. "Well, that explains it! No one gets letters from there. It's much too far away."

Janey still looked confused, but she smiled around at us, glad we were both agreeing, at least.

I closed the locket and turned it in my hand.

"Hey, what's this?" I said. There were initials on the locket. "Who's T. J. N.?"

Janey reached for the locket and paused to look at it. She pointed at the letters. "T . . . J . . . N. . . ." She looked up at me with her whole, deep smile. "That's me, Philly. Theresa Jane Nicoletto." She sat up a little straighter just to say it.

"*Theresa!*" Boomer said, and I was repeating it, too. "*Theresa* Jane?"

Janey was putting her locket back on.

I said her whole name again, just to hear it. "Theresa Jane Nicoletto. Nice name!" I was fudging a little about the Nicoletto, but I figured I'd get used to it. People with names like Philura Higley Mason can't be too particular.

"So why don't we call you Theresa?" Boomer asked.

"Yeah," I agreed, wishing I had even one decent name. "Let's call you Theresa. Or how about TJ? You'd sound more like your age, you know."

"Yeah! TJ!" Boomer chimed in.

"TJ," Janey said. But she was shaking her head.

"Why not?" we both asked.

Janey held still for a long time. She even jerked once, but went back to thinking again. Then she smiled at us.

"Because I'm Janey," she said.

2

I had to wait up late that night just to catch Mom when she wasn't working. After she finally came upstairs to get ready for bed, I kind of happened across the hall to her room.

She was standing at her bureau in her long nightgown, brushing out her dark hair. I have to admit, I still like watching Mom brush her hair. She saw me in the mirror.

"Hi, Curly Top. Lots of homework tonight?"

"Nah," I said.

I went and sat on the unused side of Mom's bed. I don't sit there very often, because it makes me think of being little, and running in on sleepy mornings to climb in with Mom and Dad (even if Dad *did* complain). Remembering how warm and right it felt being sand-wiched between two parents, I start to forget about all those years of arguments.

I guess the empty side of Mom's bed is the only sign of Dad she didn't get rid of the minute she got rid of him.

Mom was still watching me in the mirror, waiting for me to explain myself.

"You have to talk to Janey," I said.

"Is she still *up*?" Mom asked, sounding worried. She held her brush poised for a second and looked at me in the mirror.

20

"No," I said. "She's asleep." Mom went back to brushing her hair. Janey always goes to bed early. When she first came, it was hard to keep her up past seven. Mom says they didn't exactly have fun-filled evenings at Morrisville. "I don't mean talk to her now," I said. "Just sometime."

"What's up?" Mom asked. She gave her hair a few last strokes, then went to sit on her side of the bed.

"She's gotten all confused," I said. "She thinks because we have a father in Cambridge, she does, too; and did you know her real name's Theresa? *Theresa* Jane! I wish I could lose *my* first name like that."

"We can drop Philura if you want," Mom said—she was being amused—"and use *your* middle name."

"Yeah. Higley. You're a big help," I said.

"Oh, Curly Top." Mom reached over to ruffle my hair.

"But I wonder how Janey got to be Janey," I said. "There must be a reason."

Mom was setting her alarm—probably for five o'clock. "Theresa was Janey's mother's name," she said, casual, like it wasn't even news.

"You mean you know about her mother? She died, Janey says. *That* must be why they didn't use her name— too sad."

"More likely it just got confusing," Mom said, "having two Theresas in the same house."

"But her mother *died*!"

Mom was silent for only a split second, but she was *very* silent. Then she seemed to speak carefully: "Not till Janey was six."

In a flash, I could see a little-girl Janey—in pigtails—

sitting at some kitchen table while her mom checked the pie in the oven, and her dad sat smiling through his bushy mustache. I'd never imagined Janey in any family but ours. For some reason, it made my stomach kind of tighten.

"Mom! I thought you said she didn't *have* a family!"

There was that split-second silence again. Mom had shifted so I couldn't see her face. "She started out with one."

"Mom, how do you *know* all this? How come you never told me? Do you know when her father died?" Suddenly in my kitchen picture, the little-girl Janey was alone, staring out through those deep-set eyes. The tightness in my stomach was climbing to my throat, so I kept talking. "Janey showed us his picture. Have you seen it? George G. Nicoletto. Great smile—guess that's where Janey's came from. If *I* had a great dad—I mean—" I talked even faster, because I was confusing myself. "I mean, I can see why she pretends he's still alive."

Mom was straightening the books and papers on her bedside table, as if suddenly, at ten-thirty on a Thursday night, it was time to start being neat.

"Mom?"

"Janey's not pretending," she said. She turned and leaned back against the headboard, stretching her legs out on the bed. She stared at her own bare feet. "Mr. Nicoletto is still alive."

I had to hike my knee up on the bed to turn and look straight at Mom. "He's *alive*? Janey's got a father? Hey, great!" I was trying to feel happy for Janey, but instead I was filling up with questions, because how could the same person fit into two different families?

"And he actually does live in Cambridge," Mom went on. She was glaring at her feet as if they'd done something wrong.

"So how come . . . ? I mean, I thought the whole reason for Home Care . . ."

"He's not Janey's father anymore," Mom continued firmly. "Janey's part of *our* family now."

"But Janey thinks—"

"Some fathers," Mom interrupted, "don't deserve to be fathers."

Suddenly, I felt a little queasy. I'm not naive. I've heard a few sickening stories of what some fathers do to their daughters.

"You mean he *abused* her?"

This time Mom looked at me. She even sounded reassuring for a second. "Oh, no, honey, nothing like that."

I could breathe again—and see the smile on George G.'s face. "Then I don't get it," I said.

Mom was watching her toes as she curled and uncurled them. "Just take my word for it, honey. Janey's better off without Mr. Nicoletto."

"But, Mom, she acts like she *likes* him."

"What she doesn't know won't hurt her."

"What happened?" I asked. I really needed to know. I mean, when does your father stop being your father?

Mom still looked angry. "Believe me, honey, sometimes it's better to forget the past."

"*Why*, though?"

Mom sighed, and her face got softer. "Because we can't change it. That's why. And we have to move on."

I picked at the white pom-poms on her bedspread. "But maybe it could explain the reasons for some things."

Mom looked at me. "Oh, Philura," she said. I always wince when she calls me that, but she kept talking. "Knowing all the reasons in the world won't change what's already happened. Some things just are. We can't do anything about them."

"Yeah," I said. "If we could, I wouldn't be stuck being Philura."

Mom was trying not to smile. She reached to brush my hair out of my face. "But you'd still be my Curly Top," she said. "Now, come on. You've got a bus ride tomorrow. How about getting some sleep."

That was easy for *her* to say. I lay awake a long time, staring into the darkness and seeing the mustached, laughing face of George G. Nicoletto.

I figured a few things out. If Janey had a family till her mom died, it must've been George G. who put her in Morrisville. I bet that's what Mom's got against him. But I read in those books how they really *believed* back then that institutions were better. They practically *made* people send retarded kids there—even babies.

Besides, Mom calls Morrisville a warehouse and a dungeon and all, but the guy from Home Care told us Janey didn't want to leave. It took them years to convince her. She must have liked *something* about it.

My thoughts got sleepy and cloudy, but one thing stayed clear: Janey has a real, live father, same as I do. And I need to know how he fits. *Janey's* father, I mean.

3

On Dad-weekend Fridays, Mom picks us up at school. And now we stop and pick up Janey, too, outside her work program. Janey's only just learning to use the phone and all, so she doesn't stay home alone yet.

Boomer was still sulking about missing the bowling. He's always gloomy at the bus station. When we started going, he was only in first grade, and as we boarded the bus, he'd grab on to my hand before he'd let go of Mom's. I knew from April about some great places to go in Boston, so those first bus rides, I talked on and on to Boomer about making huge bubbles at the children's museum, or watching divers feed the sharks at the aquarium. He'd cheer up, but he'd still cling to my hand all the way to Dad's. Then it turned out the only places we went were pizza shacks and pancake houses. I guess when I acted all excited about that, I wasn't so convincing.

So now Boomer disappears into that music of his, and I'm the only one acting like these visits really matter.

I went outside the bus station to wait on a bench in what was left of the sun. Pretty soon, Janey came out and sat beside me.

"It's nice out here, Philly." She folded her hands in her lavender lap. "It's warm!"

"Yeah," I said. "Not bad for September."

"You're going to visit your dad again," she said. "In Cambridge."

"Right," I said. "Third weekend of every month." It was too early to mention my idea about George G., but I thought I'd start Janey thinking: "Visiting's important," I explained. "It keeps him being my dad."

Janey had her mind on something else. "How do you get there?" she asked.

I tried not to look at her. It was a funny question to ask at a bus station. But there's a lot about mental retardation I still don't understand.

"We ride on the bus," I said.

Janey smiled, but she look confused. She kind of froze for a second, then jerked to life again.

"Your mom," she started, but she paused, "Polly said *Boston*." Then she recited, "'Two tickets to Boston, round-trip.'"

Suddenly I felt really dumb. "Oh," I said. "Yeah."

Of course Janey knew we took the bus. But the only bus she ever takes is to her work program, and that goes right to the door. I never really thought about buses before. I mean, if I'd lived in the Morrisville State School all my life, buses might be hard to figure out.

"There's a bus station in Boston," I explained, "sort of like this one. Dad meets us there and drives us to Cambridge."

Janey kept smiling. I think maybe smiling was a big requirement at Morrisville.

"Some people," I added, "have to take a city bus to get

where they're going. Or these trains called subways. Or a taxi."

Janey knows about taxis. Sometimes when Mom's teaching Janey to buy her own shampoo or something, they actually take a cab. I think Mom would walk places backward on her hands before she'd use a taxi for herself, but she says Janey will need some independence someday.

Janey'd been looking at her feet, but now she looked up, all shiny teeth and sparkly eyes.

"First you go to Boston, Philly," she said. "Then you go to Cambridge."

"Right," I said, feeling almost as proud of her as she was.

Dad still meets us right at the door of the bus and thanks the driver, as if we were toddlers and the driver'd been watching out for us.

"Hi, Curly Top," Dad said, ruffling my hair.

It was warm in Boston, too, but he had on his winter hat, a knitted navy watch cap he pulls right down to his glasses. He says, being bald, it's hard to keep the heat in.

He clapped Boomer on the back, manlylike. "Hi, Sport.

"I swear you're taller every month," he added, as if Boomer could hear him over the headset. "Let's hurry. I'm parked in a tow zone." He took off in long strides through the station.

As we straggled out onto the city sidewalk, Dad reached for my canvas bag. "Share the burden," he said, grinning. He glanced at Boomer, but when Boomer packs for Dad weekends, he stuffs some underwear and maybe an extra shirt into a brown paper bag and insists on carrying it himself.

"Hey! What've you got in here?" Dad asked me. He raised and lowered the bag, testing its weight. "Machine guns? The kitchen sink?"

"Oranges," I said. "They're coming back in season." I always bring my own oranges. Dad isn't big on fresh fruit.

"I ordered sausage and black olive," he said as he unlocked the car and we got in.

"Great," I said, but it wasn't big news. Pizza is something we all agree on.

"How's school?" Dad asked.

"Okay," I said. Of course he could have been asking Boomer, but as usual, I was in the front seat and Boomer was back there listening to Mozart instead of us.

"Except maybe for Danny Stapleton," I went on. "You know that kid who was new last year? The science fair's not till May, but he's already giving me a hard time about it, just because I won. Remember I told you I won? I guess that bothered Danny. He's still trying to prove he's the smartest kid in the school." Dad smiled. "Trouble is," I added, "he's probably right." Dad chuckled and made a left turn.

"How's work?" I asked. Dad's an engineer—designs switches and things for a machine company. It's actually pretty fascinating if you can ever get him to talk about it.

"Work's work," he said. He smiled at me before he looked back at the traffic.

Even watching Dad sideways I can see how he looks

like Boomer. Or the other way around, I suppose. They've both got that big dimple in the chin, like their jaw was made of clay and someone pressed a finger into it.

"I'll just be a second," Dad said, pulling up in front of the pizza place. He left the motor running.

When he got back in, he handed the bag of sodas back to Boomer and put the pizza in my lap. There's nothing like holding a big warm box of pizza to make you eager to get where you're going.

"Welcome to my humble abode," Dad said, unlocking all the locks and pushing the door open.

I suppose humble is one word for it. It's not like Dad's poor or anything, but his apartment's just a living room and a bedroom and a bathroom. A few sports posters on the wall and yellow-brown carpet everywhere. The couch has a fold-out bed, and at first, Boomer and I both slept there. It didn't bother me, because I was only in third grade, and I knew Boomer kind of needed me, but the kid is the squirmiest sleeper. He twists and sprawls and tangles all the blankets, and never even wakes up to notice he just pushed you off the bed. So eventually, I made Dad get me my own foam mattress. He stashes it in back of the couch.

There's no kitchen in Dad's apartment—just a sink in one corner, and a hot plate, and a little stubby fridge on the floor. All he ever makes is coffee, anyway. One time, I left an orange on the counter. When I came back the next month, it was still there, all moldy with green fuzz. The whole apartment reeked.

Now all I could smell was hot pizza. I put it down on the coffee table. Boomer and I always sit on the floor, leaning over the box and shoveling the slices in. Dad sits in his E-Z Boy recliner and watches TV basketball. During meals he keeps the sound off, like he's ready for a deep conversation if anybody wants to start one.

"Let's eat," I said. "I'm starving."

We were gnawing at the last of the crusts when I guess I said something to Boomer about Janey. It must've just slipped out because she's on my mind so much. I've only told April my idea about George G. I figure Boomer will know soon enough if my research turns out right. But I hadn't meant to mention Janey.

"How long's that girl staying?" Dad asked. He startled us. Sometimes we forget he's there.

"Woman," I corrected. "Janey's practically your age, remember? But she needs to learn some things. She has to stay till she can live on her own." I was using Mom's reasons, trying to make them sound like enough.

But then Boomer added, "Janey's *family* now."

Dad sat up, and his chair sat up with him. He swiveled around to face us. "Family?" he echoed. Then he kind of laughed. "I like that! Instant family!"

"Well, you know . . ." I started.

"Yeah," Dad said. "I know, all right. That's just what family *is* to your mother. Get a little tired of one ingredient, just change the recipe! And if that doesn't cook up quite right, why, you can add one retarded girl and stir!"

"Woman," I insisted. "And anyway, we *like* Janey. She's—"

30

"And *I* like the Celtics power forward," Dad said, "but I'm not about to put him in the family album."

Sometimes it sounds like Dad is still trying to argue with Mom. I don't get it. I thought *not* arguing was the reason for being divorced.

I glanced at Boomer, thinking maybe he'd stick up for his Parcheesi buddy. But Boomer was eating the thick part of the pizza crust. He hates the thick part.

"Come on, Dad," I said, trying to lighten things up. "It's not like—" This time I was glad Dad interrupted, because I didn't have a way to finish. *I* sure can't explain why Janey fits. Especially with her father in the picture.

"I know, I know," Dad was saying. "I'm sorry, kids." He turned back toward the TV. "I know I'm not supposed to cut your mother down, but she's the one who wanted this divorce. That's just a fact." As he leaned back, the footrest shot out and raised his legs. "And as for her idea of *family* . . ."

"Hey, Dad!" I said, "Can we watch that Lakers game?"

Dad knew which one I meant.

So did Boomer. "Not *again!*" he complained.

Dad smiled at me. "You like that one, don't you, Curly Top?"

I got up and grabbed the pizza box. I crushed it hard and jammed it into the overflowing trash can in the kitchen corner. Dad rummaged through his piles of basketball tapes till he found the right one: Celtics versus Lakers, seventh and deciding game in the championship series. And the Celtics win.

Boomer had moved to the couch, and when I headed for the near end, he tried to stretch his legs so there wouldn't be room for me. But he isn't *that* tall yet. I sat down and settled in as Dad slipped the tape into the VCR. No one noticed, of course, that I slid the phone book off the end table and into my lap. Dad sighed as the game started.

It really is a good game and all, but that's not why I like it. By now, I know it by heart. I don't even watch it. I watch Dad watching it. Even after seeing it a million times, Dad can't help getting excited. At least by the third quarter, he starts jumping up out of his chair. He hollers at the screen. He slaps his knee and laughs out loud. I mean, it's just good to see him really care about something.

4

On the way back from the Pancake Palace Saturday morning, I asked to be dropped at the library. The Cambridge Public Library is smack in the middle of the high-school complex, practically across from Dad's building. I have a card, of course.

"More research?" Dad asked, smiling at me.

It wasn't exactly lying to say, "Yeah." I mean, I did actually go to the stacks first, because I might as well start looking for a science-fair topic. Even if Danny Stapleton is a jerk.

I looked at a book about soap bubbles. It's great the way they come out round no matter what shape you blow them from. I checked the book out and just stopped, sort of by-the-way, at the pay phone in the entry hall.

The phone book swiveled up from underneath the shelf. I knew the number would be there. I'd found it the night before. But sometimes it's still a big surprise to find what you're looking for:

Nicoletto Geo G 35 Winborne Cam. 854-1939

As I pushed the buttons on the pay phone, I was sort of shaking. I don't know why. I wasn't planning to talk to

George G. or anything. That's up to Janey. I just wanted to be sure he was really there so she wouldn't get all excited and then be disappointed. This time, if the guy actually answered, I figured I'd just hang up.

It rang only once.

"Hello?" He sounded *old*! Kind of croaky. I didn't hang up right away. "Hello?"

"Hi," I answered. I cleared my throat. "Uh . . . is TJ there?"

"I'm sorry, young lady." He actually *sounded* sorry. "You must have the wrong number. What number were you trying to reach?"

"Uh . . . " I'd let the phone book swivel down again. "Just a second . . . " I hauled it up and found the page and read him the number.

"You dialed right," he said, sounding proud of me. "But there's only me here. You'd better look it up again."

"Oh," I said. "Sorry to bother you."

"No bother. I'm an old man—not too busy." He sort of chuckled, and I could just see that bushy mustache.

"Okay. Thanks," I said.

"My pleasure, young lady."

I thought I could maybe really talk to him, but he hung up and left me standing there, holding the phone for no reason.

I was right. A nice guy. And he sounded pretty lonely, too. Probably just sitting around in his E-Z Boy not even realizing what a great daughter he has.

I went back to the circulation desk and got a little scrap of blue paper. I wrote out the address and the phone number carefully, in capitals, with no abbreviations.

Just outside the library, I opened the book-return box and dropped in the book about soap bubbles.

Getting off the bus back in Hampton on Sunday, I couldn't believe what I saw. It was Janey all right, but with a new turquoise coat over a new turtleneck sweater—and *real jeans*!

Mom was standing aside, trying not to look too pleased with herself.

"You look *great*, Janey!" I said, kind of shaking her shoulder, and Boomer was exclaiming, too.

"Great haircut!" I added, because it was. I mean, it wasn't the kind of hairdo I'd want, if I ever had a hairdo—kind of wavy and puffed out soft around her head—but on Janey, it fit. She looked like a teacher or something, but a nice one.

Her smile was all over her face. "Thank you, Philly. We went shopping, Philly! Polly and I. I got a skirt, Philly!"

"Fantastic!" I shook her shoulder again. I noticed she was still wearing that little-girl locket, and I was glad.

As we all headed for the car, Mom asked how our weekend was. She used to ask a hundred questions, but our answers just made her look angry, and sort of I-told-you-so, too.

Now I just say, "Fine," and that's enough for Mom.

The new clothes were a good excuse for me to just happen to be outside Janey's door that night when she came up the hall from the bathroom. She was wearing her same old pink flannel pj's.

"Hi, Philly!" She always sounds so honored to see me.

"Hey," I said. "Want to show me your new clothes?"

"Sure, Philly. I'll show you my skirt." As she went past me into her room, I could smell Ivory soap and toothpaste. I followed her, and even though Mom was still downstairs, I closed Janey's door after us. I sat on her bed, where I'd never sat before, and watched her closely.

She showed me a couple more sweaters and jeans, but then she went to her closet and unclipped a green corduroy skirt from its hanger. She held it up to her waist. "Look, Philly!" She was smiling like she owned the world.

"You'll be gorgeous!" I said. I've never seen Janey in a skirt, but smiling like that, she'd look great in a burlap bag. She even made me wonder if *I* should buy a skirt someday.

Carefully, Janey clipped her prize purchase back on its hanger. She turned around, smiling at me, but then we both looked away. It was almost as if she could tell I was there for a reason.

"Mind if I look at your locket again?" I asked.

It took her a second to realize what I meant, but then she took the beaded necklace from her bureau and handed it to me. "Sure, Philly."

I opened the little heart respectfully. There was George G. Nicoletto. I tried to match that young, laughing face with that old, croaky voice.

"Your father's still alive," I said.

"That's right, Philly." Janey seemed proud of me for getting things straight. "He lives in Cambridge, Philly." She sat down on the end of the bed and folded her hands in her lap. "Like *your* dad. And Boomer's." Her back was to me, and I could see where her pj's were worn all smooth and thin at the shoulders.

"Do you remember him?" I asked.

Janey took a breath as if to answer, then froze for a second, so the air came out in a rush. "No, Philly. I don't remember." She looked toward the dark window.

George G. was looking up at me, still laughing.

"He seems really nice," I said.

"I don't remember, Philly."

"Does he know where you live?"

"I live in Hampton, Philly. I used to live in Morrisville State School, but now I live in Hampton. With you, Philly." She twisted a little to smile over her shoulder at me.

"But I mean, does your dad know all that?"

Janey was looking at her lap. I couldn't tell anything from her back, so I just kept filling up the silence. "He seems nice, and he could really be your dad, but you have to let him know where you are!"

"I'm right here, Philly. In Hampton." She seemed to be reassuring me.

"But I mean you could call your father. And talk to him."

Janey turned to smile proudly at me. "I can call, Philly. On the telephone. Polly's teaching me."

"But don't tell Mom about this," I said quickly. "She's kind of funny about this stuff. Talking about the past, I mean. She gets all upset. So don't tell her, okay? I can help you call if you want to."

"Sure, Philly. You can help me." She still seemed to be reassuring me.

I closed the locket and got up to put it on her bureau. I

dug in my pocket for the scrap of blue paper. "Here," I said. "I wrote down his number and all. You don't have to call tonight, but sometime—whenever you want to."

Janey took the paper and pointed to the numbers. "Eight . . . five . . ." She recited George G.'s whole number, then got up to put the paper in her short-handled pocketbook. We both just stood there by the bureau.

"Hey," I said, smiling. "Before long you'll be going on the bus with Boomer and me—for a real visit!"

"Visit," Janey echoed, but she looked away, confused. She froze in thought for a long time before she said, "He doesn't visit, Philly. That's what they said. 'Janey's father doesn't visit.'"

Something yanked somewhere inside me, but I ignored it. "That was a long time ago," I said. "I've read about it, Janey. Back then, they probably *told* him not to visit. And besides, it's a long way. I mean, Morrisville's even a little farther than Hampton. Like my dad says, it's hard to get all the way out here. It's been three years, and Dad's never . . ."

I was getting off the point, and, anyway, Janey didn't seem to be listening. When I stopped, she was just jerking back from her thoughts.

"*Kathy's* father visits. And her mother, Philly. Every Sunday. Not Stevie's family. Stevie's family doesn't visit."

Janey's eyes seemed deeper than ever, and sad. Which wasn't the way I'd planned this.

"But *you* could visit," I said, all cheerful. "Wouldn't that make you happy?"

Janey looked up so suddenly, I almost backed away, but

she was smiling so her eyes got sparkly. "I'm happy, Philly. I am! I have a family, now, Philly!"

"Yeah," I said. "You do," and for a second, that seemed like all she needed. "But what about your dad?" I asked. "Don't you want a family and a father, too?"

"I have a father, Philly." She sounded almost impatient with me. "Remember? George G. Nicoletto."

She started to reach for the locket again.

"That's okay, Janey," I said. "I remember." I tried not to sound too frustrated. But what good's a father who doesn't even know you're there? I went to the door and turned with my hand on the knob. "I just wanted you to be happy," I said.

Janey took a step toward me. "I'm happy, Philly. Are you happy?"

It was a simple question, and I was about to give a simple answer, like "Sure" or "Why not?" But Janey was looking right at me, and there was kind of a burning feeling at the back of my neck, and my eyes started stinging, and I thought maybe I was going to cry. Janey looked worried, and I thought if I did cry, she'd come over and pat my back or something. She'd smell of Ivory soap and I'd feel better.

But I couldn't start crying for no reason.

I had to swallow hard to remember the simple question: "Are you happy?" was all Janey'd asked.

I rubbed my neck with both hands and said, all cheerful, "Never been happier."

I left in a hurry, but I hadn't even made it to my room before I realized I'd got it all wrong. I wasn't about to cry.

It was worse. Where I'd rubbed my neck, there were big, itchy bumps already. I stopped right there in the hall and pulled up my shirt to check my stomach. I couldn't see any bumps yet, but just looking for them made my skin burn, and I knew if I even *thought* about touching it, the bumps would spring right up. But then just trying *not* to think about it made me itch so bad, I *did* rub my stomach, and the bumps rose under my hand like horrible magic.

"Mom!" I yelled, and I wheeled around and started down the stairs. "Mom! The hives again!"

Even to myself, I sounded pretty desperate. This had happened twice before, and I'd decided if it happened again, I just wouldn't be able to stand it. But here it was, happening anyway.

Mom actually came running from her studio, and by the time she got me back upstairs, Boomer and Janey were hovering around, and my back was itching wherever my shirt touched it. I thought I was going to scream. Mom was acting supercalm, and handing me the chlor-something medicine, and I was making both my hands hold the little cup so they couldn't scratch without my telling them to. I tried to concentrate on the medicine—green, sweet, and maybe this time it would help, even though it hadn't before.

Mom asked Janey to start a cool bath and pour some oatmeal stuff into it. Boomer followed Janey, as if it were a job for two.

"Try not to panic, honey," Mom said, but when she touched my shoulder, I could feel the bumps rise, and I knew I *was* panicking, and that made me panic even more. It's not just that hives itch worse than poison ivy; it's that they *strike* like this—suddenly, for no reason—and I don't even know why, so there's nothing I can *do*. I have to stay home from school, but I can't really sleep or read, and then after a whole day of itching, when I finally decide I'll just lie in a bath for the rest of my life: Poof! The hives disappear.

The oatmeal bath did calm me down a little, and Mom went to call the advice nurse at the health plan. But we already knew what she would say: Take an antihistamine. Take a cool bath. Wait.

5

After her ballet class on Tuesday, April always knows where to find me. The Hampton Free Library has study desks they call carrels scattered all through the book stacks. There's a carrel way back by the science and ecology shelves that just sort of feels like mine.

I found some medical-type books to look up some more about hives. Before, I'd used the encyclopedia, which wasn't any more help than the doctor. "No need to worry," he says, "unless it gets hard to breathe." But there's got to be a reason for hives.

I found a diagram of skin. *Integument*, they called it, and gave the fancy names for the layers: *epidermis* on top, *dermis* under that. I was reading about "wheals of the dermis," which was the disgusting way they described hives, when April sneaked up behind my chair and put her hands over my eyes. I always know it's her. No one else is silly like that. Besides, her hands smell nice—like lotion or something.

"Hi," I said. "How're your pirouettes?"

April curved her arms and did a few whirly turns, so her gym bag swung out and whacked the end of the stacks. She ended up leaning against my carrel and smiling at me.

"Fine," she said. "How about your research?" She tossed her head a little, and her hair just fell into place—all soft and brushed back, like there's a little sunny breeze across her cheek.

"Maybe I'll do hives for the science fair," I said. "I could be my own exhibit. Danny Stapleton would love it!"

"Hey, did I tell you his brother's in June's history class?" June is April's sister; she's in high school.

"Lucky June," I said.

"Actually, she says Frank's okay. But, anyway, what about the hives? Any new clues?"

"Yup! It's definitely emotional stress."

"Yeah, right," April said, knowing I'd have to smile. I'm not exactly the stressed-out type. In fact, it's hard to find anything that bothers me. Except for hives, of course.

"So it's got to be allergies," I concluded. "But it's not like I started eating octopus—or peanut butter and ketchup or anything!"

April thought for a minute. "Hey! What about the other night—that stuff Janey made, that tofu concoction." There's something about her dad being a writer that makes April like to use big words.

"Tofu-cheese squares," I said. "But they're not really new. Mom's just teaching Janey some easy meals."

"They were good," April said.

"I know. Janey's amazing, learning to use the blender and all." I looked down and closed the integument book carefully. "But she doesn't understand about fathers."

April sighed. "Just 'cause she won't call?"

I stacked the medical books in a neat pile. "She doesn't

even *remember* him! Can you imagine what that's like, having a father who doesn't even *know* you anymore?"

"No," April said, which was probably just the truth. *Her* dad has long talks with her, and hugs her like it's no big deal. Maybe April doesn't understand about fathers, either.

"Well, *I* can sure imagine it," I said, but I sounded almost angry, so I stopped, and swallowed, and folded my hands on the stack of books. "I just want Janey to be happy," I said.

April shrugged. "Maybe she already is."

Things seem simple to April.

I tried to explain. "She can't be *really* happy if her father's not being her father." Something in my voice still didn't sound right. I tried to shrug like April, and I added, all cheerful, "But that's okay!" Someone came near us in the stacks, and my voice lowered to a whisper automatically. "Janey can learn *lots* of things she never learned before. I bet I can help her understand. We *have* to keep in touch, or else . . . " My voice got so quiet it just faded out.

April pulled a chair from another carrel and sat sideways, so I was looking at her profile. Even just hanging out, she holds her head like a dancer.

"You only just found out about George G.," she whispered, "but you're already . . . " She didn't go on.

"What?" I prodded.

"Well it's like last year—the science fair. All you could talk about was rain. Rain this and rain that. Even on sunny days. And now it's Janey and George G. It's like—I don't know—it's like you're obsessed or something."

Obsessed is one word I wish April hadn't learned. Coming out in a whisper like that, it sounded like a hissing snake.

"Well, your dad's *always* around," I said. The person left the stacks and my voice got louder. "Some of us have to work at it, that's all." I thought I was kidding April, but it didn't sound that way.

She looked a little hurt. "Come on, Philly! All I mean is Janey could have her own reasons."

She said it casually, like nothing important, when I was taking in air to say more.

I let out my breath like a balloon going flat. Why hadn't I thought of that? "You're right," I said to April. "Like those cards she carries. Janey can have her own reasons." I decided then and there to forget about George G. "I'm really dumb," I mumbled.

April laughed. "Yeah, right. Dumb and stressed out— that's you, Philly!" She stood up, shoving her chair back into place. "Come on. I'm hungry. You got anything good at your house?"

As I went to put the medical books away, April grabbed my jacket and followed me. "I mean, anything besides oranges?" she added. She smiled and held out my jacket.

"Thanks," I said. "And we might have some crackers."

We came out of the stacks into what I call the banquet room, because of the long tables in rows. A few lone people were bent over newspapers and books. Our voices went hushed again.

"No cheesecake?" April asked, teasing. Cheesecake's the kind of thing we get at her house, because her dad's got a sweet tooth and likes to cook.

"Dream on!" I said. Then I grinned. "But I'm sure

Boomer'd be glad to fix you his favorite kind of sandwich."

"Thanks, but no thanks! I'll take the crackers."

Even though we never have cheesecake, April comes to our house a lot. It's like she just belongs—"practically family," Mom calls her. It's different when I go to April's. They're *really* a family. I can tell, because I don't fit. They have a round kitchen table that's always set for four. When they set an extra place for me, I'm squashed against the table leg.

April had gone ahead to pull open one of the big front doors. She grinned at me. "After you!"

"Hey, April," I said as I passed her, "your integument's showing!"

The Hampton Free Library has a set of grand stairs in front, so walking out the door is like stepping onto a stage. Especially when the sun's out, which it still was.

April just stopped on the top step while I started down. I looked back, grinning, and she was standing there with her hands on her hips. "Okay, Philura *H*. Mason," she said. She didn't have to talk quietly anymore, and she put a lot of emphasis on the *H*, like she might yell out my middle name, right there in the middle of town. "What's teguwhatsis?" She wouldn't budge one inch till I told her; I knew that.

"Integument," I repeated. "Yours is showing—*wow*, is it ever showing!"

April just folded her arms across her puffy blue jacket and waited. Standing there all high and mighty, she was having to work not to smile.

"Don't worry, though," I said. "The librarian's was showing, too." I was really cracking myself up, and April started laughing just because I was.

"Sometime today," she said, meaning I'd better hurry up and tell her. I went back up the steps and hooked my elbow around hers. "Skin," I said. "Your skin is show-ing." She pushed me away, but then started walking down with me.

"Integument?" she asked.

"You've got it!"

Then April grinned at me. "In fact," she added, "I've got it all over!"

JANUARY

6

I've been working hard on the science fair—at least, on finding a topic. Way back in October, I started with the *A* volume of the encyclopedia, and I'm going right through the alphabet till I find what I want to work on. I just leaf through the pages, not stopping unless I'm really interested in something, but the trouble is, I'm interested in too much. I want to know the reasons for lots of things—like albinos and blushing and camouflage and dreams and erosion. Here it is January, and I'm only up to *E*. Danny Stapleton likes to stop by my carrel and gloat. He acts as if *his* secret topic's going to win him the Nobel Prize.

When April has ballet after school, we stop at the bottom of the library steps. This time, we didn't stop for long, because the wind was nasty cold.

"Hope you make it to *F*," she said, only smiling a little. Now she thinks I'm obsessed about science-fair topics.

"Yeah, and good luck with your arabesques," I said.

When she was a few steps away and I was a few steps up, she added, "I'll call you about the allergy doctor, okay?"

"Sure," I called back. "See you tomorrow."

I'd only just finished *E* before I had to be out on the steps again, waiting for Mom. At least that meant leaving before Danny showed up. I had an appointment about the hives. They keep coming back. Every few weeks. And even after scratch tests, we still don't have a clue.

Doctors sure are big on the reasons for things. All this one did was ask a million questions. She thought the hives were just a new reaction to something that never used to bother me. She was looking for patterns, she said. "For example, you seem to get these hives toward the end of every month. Maybe that's significant. Maybe not." She paused. "I have to warn you," she added, "the cause of hives usually goes undetected. But we can try." She said I should get a little date book to keep track of everything I eat, and exactly when the hives strike, and how long they last.

On the way home, Mom stopped at a stationery store so I could buy the date book. Then she had to drop off a change of clothes for Janey. Now that Janey's in this food-service training program, she wears a uniform every day. A friend had invited her to go to a movie after work, and she wanted to wear that green corduroy skirt.

I've never mentioned George G. again, and neither has Janey. She still wears her locket and carries that mixed-up pack of cards, but otherwise it's like her whole life started in our family.

Mom parked by a big factory-looking building, and I figured, rather than wait in the cold car, I'd go in and say hi to Janey. We had to walk through a maze of short hallways, all slanted downward like ramps, till we got to the back of the building. Then we came out into a big, noisy open space that was set up with tables and chairs, like a café.

I have to admit, I wasn't prepared. I hadn't thought about it or anything. There were all these retarded people there. I mean, I've read about lots of different reasons—heredity, and brain damage, and just being neglected—but there're probably only two retarded kids in our entire school. This was like a whole different world. Everyone was sitting around talking and laughing. A couple of people were in wheelchairs. It looked like coffee-break time. Several people had noticed us, and suddenly I couldn't think what to do with my hands.

"Hi, Polly," one man called. He kind of slurred it, so it sounded like *Powy*. "TJ's 'n th' kitchen."

I was starting to wonder who TJ was, when I realized the guy meant Janey.

"Thanks, Kevin," Mom said.

I could see the kitchen beyond a serving counter with a cash register on it. Mom headed that way, and I followed, trying to look straight ahead. I've never been in a foreign country, but that's what it felt like, and I didn't have a clue how to act. I couldn't believe Janey came here every day and I'd never even imagined it.

Lots of people said hi to Mom. "TJ's working," they'd add, or "TJ leaving early?" Since when was Janey TJ? It was like she had a secret identity, a whole secret life.

I hung back a little and watched Janey greet Mom. "Hi, Polly. How are you, Polly?" Janey's white uniform made her look like a nurse, except for the black trim and the hair net. "I'll get you some mint tea. Right, Polly?"

53

Then she saw me and her smile widened. "Hi, Philly! You came, too! This is where I work, Philly. Every day!"

"Yeah," I said. I crooked my arm and kind of wiped the air with the flat of my hand. It was supposed to be a wave, but it just felt dumb. "Hi, Ja—" I swallowed. She wasn't even Janey anymore.

"Wait, Philly," she said. She went to a huge fridge in the back. She had to use both hands on the big lever handle, but it only took her a minute to find what she was after. She came back, looking proud of herself, and handed me an orange.

"Thanks," I said, really meaning it.

"You like oranges," Janey said. "I know that, Philly."

Janey poured herself a cup of coffee. I watched her closely. She seemed so comfortable here—as if this was more home than our house.

After Mom paid for us, we went to sit with Kevin. Kevin had Down's syndrome. I'm not sure how I could tell, but I read about it in the D volume—some tiny extra chromosome in one little gene. Except the encyclopedia pictures were of little kids—like the girl I've seen in the first grade. Wide, soft faces. Cute. Kevin looked like a really nice guy, but he wasn't particularly cute. He had graying hair, and he wore glasses, and he was pudgy like Danny Stapleton. He blinked a lot as Mom introduced me.

"Kevin, this is my daughter, Philura."

"Philly," I corrected.

"Hi, Philly," he said, making it sound like *Phiwy*. His smile crinkled his eyes. Then he stuck out his hand to shake mine. "TJ tol' me 'bout you." He sounded kind of like his mouth was full, and I remembered that Down's syndrome makes a person's tongue a little thicker.

Janey sat down next to Kevin, and Mom asked what movie they were going to.

That's when it clicked that this was the friend who'd invited Janey out. Janey was going on a date. I shouldn't have been so surprised. I mean, Janey's a grown-up, and she doesn't have to tell me everything, but I *am* supposed to be family. April's only sort of family, and I hear *lots* about her sister June's dates. I thought I knew Janey, that's all.

Mom and Janey and Kevin were talking on. I was the only stranger in that whole, noisy room. I peeled my orange, but the first section didn't taste right, so I sat there fiddling with it and getting all sticky with juice.

Mom was figuring out with Janey how she'd get home—maybe call from Kevin's group home, or actually take a taxi by herself. Then Kevin put his arm around the back of Janey's chair. I mean, just naturally, like maybe I'd push my hair out of my face. Janey kept talking to Mom but kind of leaned into Kevin's arm, the way I've seen June do when she and her boyfriend are supposedly studying in the library.

I didn't even think about what I said next. I wish now I had, but I didn't. I just leaned forward, grinning.

"Janey," I said, and she turned and smiled at me like she was just glad I was there. "That uniform looks great," I said, "but your integument's showing."

I could feel Mom look at me really hard, but I kept on grinning at Janey. The smile stayed on her face. The smile stayed right there, the same size and shape and everything. It just kind of hung there on Janey's face while Janey crumpled behind it. I mean, she kind of shriveled away from Kevin and slumped into herself, and her hands hesitated over the table and then fluttered toward her face and then her lap, like they were trying to figure out what to cover up. She looked back at me, kind of pleading, while the smile just stayed on her face.

I was still grinning like an idiot. "Skin," I said. "Your skin is showing." It seemed like her eyes just filled up with questions, and I didn't have one single answer. My grin had gone all stiff. I actually had to swipe at it to make it go away. "It was a joke," I said. "A really lame one."

No one said anything for a second. Kevin took a napkin and leaned over toward Janey to wipe up a little coffee spill. I didn't dare even glance at Mom. I could tell she was wound up ready to explode as soon as she got me alone.

"I'm sorry, Janey," I said, but it didn't change a thing.

Janey still looked slumped when Mom finally handed her the green corduroy skirt and a blouse, and we got out of there.

Mom couldn't even talk. We got into the car and she just sat there, gripping the steering wheel and glaring at the middle of it, as if she had to concentrate hard to keep from killing me.

"How *dare* you!" she said at last. She was too tightened up to even yell. "That was *cruel*, Philura Mason. *Cruel!* There's just no other word for it!"

"Nasty," I mumbled. "Mean." I wasn't being sassy. I'd been thinking of some words myself.

Finally, Mom started the car. "What on earth got into you?" She scowled at the traffic as she pulled out into it. I turned to stare out my side window.

"April thought it was funny," I said, knowing what a weak excuse that was.

"April," Mom repeated. "The most secure, well-adjusted kid in Hampton." She went silent again.

"I didn't mean to," I mumbled, but the trouble was, I *had* meant to. For a minute, I had *wanted* to hurt Janey, and I didn't even know the reason.

I heard Mom take a deep breath, but she didn't let it out. "I thought you *liked* Janey," she said. "I thought you actually *cared* about her." I thought so, too, so I wasn't full of arguments. "What did Janey ever do to you?"

"Moved in," I said before I even thought it. "Moved in for no reason."

"Don't give me that, Philura Higley Mason." At least Mom was raising her voice now. "You liked Janey from the start."

That's exactly what I mean, I wanted to say, but the words were too far inside me. How could someone fit so well and still be able to leave?

Mom was silent again, same as I was, but I could feel her glance at me a few times. Then she sighed like her teakettle losing steam. I guess she noticed the tears on my face. I was just noticing them myself, and I was probably more surprised than she was. I never cry.

"What's the matter, Philura?" Mom said. She still didn't sound very sympathetic, which made plenty of sense to me.

I swiped at my face. "I don't know," I said. It was true.

I didn't know anything anymore. I mean, how can people just come and go from a family for no reason?

It wasn't Janey's fault. That much I could figure out.

"I'm sorry, Mom," I said.

Mom reached out and patted my knee. "I know you are, Curly Top. Don't worry. Janey's survived a lot worse."

It wasn't exactly comfort, but I guess it was the best Mom could do.

That night when April called, I told her about the date book, but not about Janey. Then I sat on my bed in my nightshirt and made myself keep looking in the closet-door mirror: those skinny arms and legs, the mess of curls. Pretty bad, but I still couldn't see where the meanness came from. Boomer kind of happened into my room and told me about a unit on magnets they're doing. I guess he was hinting I could do magnets for the science fair, but I couldn't act very enthusiastic.

Finally I heard Janey get home and come up to her room. I let her have a minute, and then I went and knocked on her door.

She opened it and smiled. She did look great in that corduroy skirt. "Hi, Philly. I'm home now, Philly." I couldn't tell if her smile was any thinner than usual.

"Can I come in a sec?"

"I was putting it away," Janey said, and I realized she was holding some ten-dollar bills. She gets a monthly check from social security, and Mom's taught her to put some in the bank, but Janey wants to *see* her money, too. She keeps a big pile of tens in her top bureau drawer and transfers a few to her pocketbook whenever she needs cash.

Janey went back to her open bureau drawer, and I sat on a chair, feeling formal.

"I'm really sorry," I said, "—about my stupid joke. It was mean. Kevin seems nice. Did you have a good time?"

Janey didn't even pause. "I had a good time, Philly. I bought popcorn. And I took a taxi, Philly. All by myself!"

I took a deep breath. "I like you a lot, Janey."

Janey smiled. "I like you, too, Philly."

I spoke in a rush. "I don't know why I got mean, but I think it's maybe *because* I like you—and I know that doesn't make any sense but . . . " I paused. I folded my hands. "I guess I'm having trouble understanding some things."

Janey smiled, more sparkly than ever. "Like me, Philly," she said. "*I* have trouble understanding things, too!"

7

Right near the beginning of the *F* encyclopedia there's a whole big spread about "Family." They call it "the oldest human institution" and "an adventure in cooperation" and all, but I notice they're sort of hedging the whole time. They never really say what makes a family a family. I mean, when you look up hives, you find out what they *are*. You can tell if that's what you've got or not.

I was looking at the pictures of families all over the world when I heard Danny Stapleton coming. I knew it was him without looking around. Danny wears these high-top sneakers without ever tying them up, so he kind of sloshes when he walks. He's a little bit pudgy, and sort of pigeon-toed, and the only time he *doesn't* look like a jerk is if you happen to catch him reading or something and he doesn't know anybody's watching. Then, I have to admit, he looks as smart as he thinks he is.

I flipped the encyclopedia pages to another heading— "Fungi"—and pretended not to notice Danny. He stopped right near me and said, "Hi, Philura." I could tell he was smiling. Actually, Danny *never* smiles. He only grins.

I acted like I was reading something fascinating. "Fungi . . . ," I muttered, "the lowest division of the plant kingdom."

"Hey, Philura!" Danny said, a little louder.

If I didn't look up, he'd stay there saying "Philura" louder and louder till everyone in Hampton heard it. I looked up.

"Yes, Daniel?" Whenever I call Danny *Daniel*, he just grins wider, like there's some joke he's not telling.

"Watcha doing for the science fair, Philura?" The wider Danny grins, the pudgier his cheeks get.

"It's still January," I said, trying to sound all scornful. "The science fair's not till May."

I swear Danny can actually puff himself up. Not just his chest, either. It's like there's extra air right down to his toes. "Genuine scientific inquiry," he said, acting extremely serious, "requires lengthy planning, as well as in-depth research. It's never too soon to establish a focus." Then he deflated and grinned again.

"Give me a break," I said, being careful not to smile.

Danny sounded like a superpatient teacher. "Take all the time you need, Philura. *I* chose a topic three months ago, so *my* research is well under way. If you need help, I'd be happy to give you a little of my valuable time."

"Stinking smut," I said, reading the caption on a photo of wheat fungus.

Danny peered over my shoulder at the encyclopedia. "Fungi," he said. "Fascinating." He was still trying to sound all superior, but I could tell some of the pictures had caught his eye. We were both starting to notice how fungi actually are pretty interesting. There're some that look like umbrellas, and some that look like little birds' nests with eggs in them. I turned the page and we looked for a second at a beautiful, frilly white mushroom that the caption said was deadly poisonous.

"Bioluminescence," Danny read from the "Related Articles" list. He pretended it wasn't a question.

"When they glow in the dark," I said, remembering from the B volume. "Like fireflies, I guess, only fungi don't flash."

"Oh, yeah," Danny said. "Hey, and my mom showed me this article about a forty-acre fungus. Or maybe even bigger, I think. It was pretty amazing!"

Danny was forgetting himself.

"And look at all these great names," I said. "'Cedar apple' and 'slime mold' and 'potato scab.'"

Danny leaned closer, but then he caught himself. He stood back and cleared his throat. "Enough of this idle distraction," he said.

"Thinking of changing your topic?" I asked.

Danny found his grin again. "Genuine scientific inquiry—"

"Yeah, I know," I interrupted. "Focus." I focused carefully on the fungi and added, "Bye, Danny."

"Good day, Philura. Don't strain your brain!"

He'd only sloshed a few steps when I said, "Hey, Danny!" He turned, surprised, and I looked him straight in the eye. "Your integument's showing!"

Danny didn't even blink. "So's yours," he said. "So's everybody's," and he disappeared around the stacks.

I went home a little early. April was doing something with her dance friends, and, anyway, I wasn't getting any closer to genuine scientific inquiry.

Taking off my jacket in the front hall, I could hear Mom talking in the kitchen. The other voice belonged to Rich, Janey's caseworker from Home Care. For a second, I was afraid he'd come to move Janey because of my being so nasty. But when I went into the kitchen, he just said hello and kept talking. Boomer was there, just putting the peanut butter and ketchup away. He adjusted his headset and grabbed his sandwiches and headed for his room. He waved at me as if I was somewhere in the distance. Mom and Rich didn't seem to mind when I got an orange and sat down at the table to peel it.

"She's been asking about it a lot," Rich was saying. "And I think she's ready." Rich is a sort of barrel-shaped guy with lots of dark hair and a beard. He talks really deep, like the papa bear in cartoons.

"We just got her away from all that," Mom said.

Rich nodded. "She's adjusted remarkably well. But she hasn't forgotten. Not TJ. She—"

"Hey," I interrupted. "Excuse me, but when *I* suggested TJ, she told me not to call her that."

"Aaah," said Rich, like someone making a big discovery. "So *you're* the one who suggested it. About September-October, right? She suddenly wanted folks to call her TJ. It's great—a much more adult-sounding name—but we wondered where she got it."

"But she told *me* to call her Janey."

Mom smiled. "That's because you're family. Imagine if Aunt Noreen got called Nolly at work! What amazes me is how Janey picks up on these things."

"Yeah," I said. "Faster than I do."

Rich chuckled. "But that's just my point. TJ's unusual.

Let me see, she's been here . . . " He started flipping through some papers he had in a folder.

"Eight months," I said, and Rich glanced at me before he went on.

"Eight months," he said to Mom. "And look how much she's learned, how well she's settled in. If she wants this, I'm sure she's ready." He leaned back in his chair, eyeing my orange. "That smells great. Could I have a section?"

"You want a whole one?" I asked, but he didn't. Lucky Boomer wasn't there. He knows I never give away bites of my orange. It's not that I can't share. If there's only one orange, someone else can have it. But if the orange is mine, I want the whole thing.

"Janey hasn't said a word about this to *me*," Mom said.

Rich popped my orange section into his mouth. "Knowing TJ"—he wiped some juice from his beard— "she could probably tell how you'd react." He smiled at Mom, but Mom wasn't smiling.

"Hey," I asked, "what's this all about, anyway?"

Mom reached for one of my orange peels and started breaking it into pieces.

Rich answered. "Janey wants to go back to Morrisville."

My heart jumped. My jaw froze in the middle of chewing. This was my fault.

"For a visit," Rich continued, like it was obvious.

I could swallow again, but I still felt awful jumpy. I glanced at Mom. That orange peel was in tiny pieces.

"Why remind her of all that misery?" Mom said.

Rich leaned toward her, folding his hands on his papers. "It wasn't *all* misery, Polly."

"No," said Mom. "I suppose not." I wondered if Rich

knew the warning signs in that tone of Mom's—ever so slightly sarcastic. She was winding up for a good argument. "I suppose not," she said again. "I suppose even at the Morrisville State School for the Mentally Retarded, every once in a while"—Mom talked faster and faster—"say, maybe every five years or so, the sun came into the dayroom in just the right way to make a rainbow on the wall, and maybe one or two of those times, somebody just happened to stop rocking and moaning in a corner to brush a fly away and saw the rainbow. No," she said, leaning back hard, "I suppose it wasn't *all* misery."

Rich signed. "TJ—" he started. He glanced at me and smiled. "*Janey* wasn't rocking and moaning in a corner, Polly. She had friends there. She didn't want to leave at first. That institution was her life."

"Life!" Mom said. "You call that a life? Locked up with hundreds of other people that nobody bothered to care about just because they weren't perfect like the rest of us! You call that a *life*? Being bored silly because nobody figured there was any point in teaching you anything, since you were just going to be there, rotting in the dayroom and then being locked into your cottage at night!"

Rich and I were both just kind of staring at Mom by now. She sure was angry at something, but it wasn't obvious what.

"Mom," I said, trying to remind her to calm down.

She brushed her little collection of orange peels from the table into her palm and stood up to throw them in the trash.

Rich watched her till she sat back down. He turned to me, but I could tell it was still Mom he was talking to.

"Even when folks don't want to go back, we encourage them to, in time. It's their past. Part of them. They need to accept it—and so do we."

This was getting extremely interesting. I was careful not to look at Mom. I had a feeling she wouldn't lecture *Rich* about forgetting the past and moving on.

I was right. No one interrupted Rich, which seemed to suit him just fine. He was sounding more and more like some preacher.

"You see, people used to think you could block out the past—forget it, and it wouldn't affect you. Now we know that doesn't work." I just *had* to sneak a look at Mom. She was rubbing at some ink stains on her hands. "In fact," Rich went on, adjusting himself in his chair, "that's how folks like TJ ended up in the state school in the first place—their parents were told to forget."

I'd been careful not to think of George G. for a long time. But now his smiley picture was clear in my mind, and so was his sad, croaky voice.

I knew Mom might kill me later, but I absolutely *had* to ask. I focused carefully on Rich. "What about Janey's father?"

I expected Mom to jump, but she didn't. She just sighed as Rich glanced at her. He seemed to have gotten permission to answer.

"Once, about ten years ago," he said slowly, "TJ got pneumonia—real bad. They thought she was dying. The institution called her father." Rich glanced at Mom again before he went on, gently. "He told them not to call again. He didn't want to know. Either way. He didn't care if Janey lived or died."

I sat there for maybe a whole minute before I could even react. Then I seemed to tighten all over, as if the hives were starting, but inside. I got scared. I'm not used to feeling like killing anyone, but all of a sudden I wanted like crazy to go find Mr. George G. Nicoletto and strangle him. I looked at Mom, and I admit I felt kind of desperate. It was awful, feeling so mad. I guess Mom had some clue, because she put her hand on my knee and looked into my eyes. She hadn't said a word during all Rich's preaching, but now she took a long, deep breath and let it out slowly.

"Want to go with us?" she asked me.

"Where?" I said. For a second I thought maybe there really was a plan to go and strangle George G.

Mom sat up straight and folded her hands on the table. "To the Morrisville State School for the Mentally Retarded," she said. "If Janey wants to go, we should be there. Boomer, too. We'll go as a family."

8

We couldn't go to Morrisville right away because of the January Dad weekend. Boomer and I rode the bus to Boston in a mess of cold rain and slush. There weren't any bowling parties or birthday parties or chamber music concerts for Boomer to be missing, so he sulked about the weather.

I ignored him for a while, but there was something about the gloomy rain and the way the bus seemed dark and quiet inside: I felt like we were driving into a tunnel, and the closer I got to Cambridge, the deeper the tunnel was getting. I wanted the bus to jam into reverse and back me out of there, but it just kept going. I tried to picture Dad—waiting for us, smiling—but the guy I kept *seeing* was George G. All there was at the end of the tunnel was a father who'd stopped caring about his daughter. I wanted to blow him to pieces, but the closer I got, the more it felt like being that angry would blow *me* to pieces instead.

I looked over at Boomer. He had his headset on and his eyes closed and his face turned toward the ceiling. It was as if I could actually *watch* some beautiful passage of music float across his face.

But he also still smelled of peanut butter and ketchup. I shook his shoulder. I figured the least he could do was carry on a conversation.

"What?" he said, annoyed, but he took off his headset I noticed he pressed PAUSE, not OFF.

"I was thinking about Janey," I said. "And Morrisville."

"Yeah? So?"

He was still trying to act obnoxious, but I knew I'd grabbed him. Janey's special to Boomer, too—she's the only member of this family who never gets mad at him for being like he is: moody, I mean, and hiding inside that headset. When Mom told Boomer about the Morrisville plan, he looked at her like she was crazy. But because Janey was there, he only nodded and agreed to go.

"How bad could it be?" I said now.

"Yeah," Boomer said.

"I mean, Janey *wants* to go."

"Yeah."

"But . . . " I started.

"But Mom acts like . . . " he started.

"Yeah," I agreed. "Like it's a swamp there or something."

"Quicksand," Boomer said.

"Yeah, quicksand. Like it could suck Janey back and she'd be stuck forever."

"Mom's weird sometimes," Boomer said, and we both smiled.

I noticed him push the OFF button on his tape player. I took a deep breath and let it out slowly so it wouldn't sound like a sigh. I let the back of my seat down a notch and took out an orange.

"Can I have a section?" Boomer asked, as if he'd only just met me.

I handed him another whole orange, but he just tossed it back and forth between his hands a few times, thinking.

"How bad *could* it be?" he asked.

We made up horror scenes about Morrisville, with ghosts and Janey-eating monsters and a weird mist that gave us all hives forever. Then we made up paradise scenes, where Janey loved Morrisville so much that we all just moved back there with her. We got laughing, and the tunnel feeling went away, and Boomer didn't put his headset back on till we were almost to Boston.

I got out my date book to record the orange I'd just eaten. I know oranges can't be the reason for my hives, or I'd have hives all the time, but the doctor said to write down everything.

The trouble is, whenever I open that book, I start feeling prickly. It's like I'm just *waiting* for my neck to start itching. It was especially bad this time. "Toward the end of every month," the doctor'd said, so I was afraid the problem was something I eat at Dad's. Looking for a clue, I wrote down what supper was going to be: "Pizza, sausage and black olives, three slices; one can orange soda."

Then I listed the whole weekend: Saturday morning French toast at the Pancake Palace, deli sandwiches for lunch, take-out Chinese Saturday night; then the Pancake Palace for Sunday brunch, and probably grilled cheese at the bus station before we left. Nothing weird. Nothing new.

But at least I wouldn't have to open the date book so much.

It really was Dad waiting at the door of the bus. Blue watch cap, glasses, dimple in the chin. No resemblance to George G. Nicoletto.

"I ordered sausage and black olive," Dad said as we got into the car.

"Great!" I said, but I couldn't help wondering if it was Cambridge pizza that was causing my hives.

"How's school?" he asked.

I told him about trying to find a science-fair topic and about how Danny Stapleton likes to gloat. Dad chuckled and ruffled my hair.

"So how's work?" I asked.

"Well," Dad said, "pretty much the same." But he kind of trailed off, as if maybe there was more.

I leaned forward and looked at him. He glanced at me and smiled. "They're sending me to San Francisco next week. Guess they need some help out there."

"Hey! Great!" I said. Every so often, Dad's machine company sends him places, like he's the only engineer in the country who can solve some little design problem. "Did you hear that, Boomer?" I said, twisting around a little. "David R. Mason to the rescue!"

"Yeah," Boomer said, pretending he knew what we were talking about.

"So what's got them stumped this time?" I asked Dad.

He smiled, but shrugged. "Just some little technical hitch," he said. He was pulling up in front of the pizza place. "I'll just be a second." And he splashed out into the slush.

After the take-out Chinese Saturday night, I had to check my date book to make sure I'd remembered the fortune cookies.

"Keeping a diary?" Dad asked, turning a little from his game.

I explained to him about the hives, but I felt so prickly, I had to fold my hands to keep them from finding someplace to scratch.

"You don't get hives from *my* side of the family," Dad said. "Thick skins. Every one of us." He chuckled. "In the case of my parents, rhinoceros hides."

I handed him a fortune cookie. I didn't much want to hear about his parents again. They both died before I was born, and about the only thing I know about them is how they made Dad work his own way through college because he didn't want to be a doctor like they both were.

Dad just put his fortune cookie on the arm of his E-Z Boy.

"Hey!" I said. "You have to open it!"

He tossed it back to me. "You can do the honors."

I don't really believe in fortune cookies, of course. Mine had been something about traveling far and wide for business and pleasure, and Boomer's was about his "mentality" being "alert and practical." So I read Dad's aloud, glancing at Boomer and getting ready to laugh.

"'Strengthen ties to family.'"

The only laugh was a kind of snort from Dad. I wished I'd checked the thing first.

"Family," Dad said. He actually sounded sad for a second. He was holding the remote and idly pushing buttons, but the remote was facing him, so nothing changed. Then he laughed again. "What family?"

I looked over at Boomer, who was looking at me. Weren't *we* supposed to be family?

72

"Give that one to your mother," Dad said. "Or that Janey of yours. She's family now, right?"

"Come on, Dad," I said. "She really needs us. I mean, *her* father—" But then I filled up so fast with anger, I had to breathe hard to calm down. How could a father just decide not to be a father? "Dad," I started again, but what was I planning to say? I crumpled the fortune and started gathering up all the cartons and little packets of sauce. I put everything—leftovers and all—back into the bag and set it on the floor by the overflowing trash can. If I put the leftovers in the fridge, they'd still be there when we came next month.

Boomer had put his headset on. I had to admit he was probably being smart not to stick up for Janey this time, but he still made me mad. I put my date book back into my canvas bag and sat down on the couch. I looked at Dad. He was leaning forward with his elbows on his knees.

I swallowed very carefully. "Hey, Dad," I said, all cheerful. "Can we watch that Lakers game?"

I guess Boomer didn't hear me, because he didn't even groan.

Dad stood up to get the tape. He smiled at me. "You like that one, don't you, Curly Top?"

All that worrying and recording didn't do me any good. The hives still struck when I got home. Lying in that oatmeal bath trying not to scream, I just about decided all I'd ever eat at Dad's again would be oranges, oranges, oranges.

Oranges are something I can trust.

9

It was the very end of January when we actually went to Morrisville.

We'd had a big snowstorm, and it was pretty when we drove up the long driveway—all open spaces, and big, spreading trees still trimmed with white. It was like the college campus in Hampton, only not even trampled. The snow at Morrisville was smooth and perfect.

"Does anybody still live here?" Boomer asked. He'd left his headset at home.

"Not more than a hundred, I guess," Mom answered. "It'll close for good before long." She sounded somehow relieved.

Janey was silent. Getting ready to come, she'd been excited. She'd dressed in her corduroy skirt, but she'd also brought that mismatched pack of cards, carefully nestled into her old short-handled pocketbook.

I was sitting in the backseat, right behind her, so I couldn't see her face. I poked Boomer and cocked my head toward Janey, raising my eyebrows to make it a question. He smiled and put both thumbs up.

But *he* couldn't see Mom. She looked awful. She kept glancing at Janey, and swallowing so hard I could see her throat jump. It spooked me.

Finally, Janey burst out, "That's my cottage, Polly," and

Mom was already parking. "Cottage C," Janey said. "I lived there, Polly."

"*Cottage?*" Boomer asked, and he had a point: It was more like a big brick house, and there wasn't any white picket fence or anything. Just a wooden sign with strips all pointing in different directions: ADMINISTRATION, INFIRMARY, COTTAGES D–F, TAFT BUILDING. All the paths were paved and black, with sharp-cut edges from a snowblower.

Janey got out of the car and smiled—proudly, it seemed—at Boomer and me. "Come on, Boomer," she said, and "I'll show you my room, Philly."

We all followed her up the front walk. She was carrying that old red pocketbook like a brimming bucket. I guess I expected her to ring or knock, but she just opened the door and walked in.

It was quiet inside and smelled of cigarettes. We could see into a sort of living room. There was a guy sitting in there with a pile of thick books next to him, but he wasn't studying, just sitting there smoking.

"Nobody'll be back till after lunch," he called to us.

Mom went over and explained why we were there. She asked if we could look around. It didn't seem to matter to him.

Janey led us up the stairs. Our feet slapped and echoed on the rubber treads, then clattered down the linoleum hall. Janey stopped a few doors down and pointed at the room number.

"Two-one-four," she recited. "Cottage C, room two-one-four. This is my room, Polly."

I noticed she didn't say "was," but she should have.

When she opened the door, we could see that the room was bare. It still had two beds and two bureaus in it, but it was bare.

Janey froze with her arms crooked in front of her. Suddenly I realized she hadn't been doing that so much lately. She froze for what seemed like ages. Boomer went to look out the window, but Mom and I just stood there, as frozen as Janey.

"Kathy's gone," Janey said at last.

Mom's words spilled out like they'd been piled up behind a dam. "Was Kathy your roommate? She's got a new home, too, I bet. I could probably find her if you want me to. What's her last name?"

Janey was still, then jerked to life. "Kathy's parents visit," she said. "Every Sunday, Polly." I'd heard that before, along with "Janey's father doesn't visit," but back then, I hadn't understood.

Mom seemed lost for words. I wanted to feel angry at George G. again, but instead there was this big, drowning sadness filling me up to where it scared me. I wanted to grab Janey by the wrist and yank her right out of there. I wanted to take her home.

But Janey smiled and added, "Kathy likes pickles, Polly."

We were all pretty quiet till we got outside again.

"Want to go home now, Janey?" Mom asked. She already had her keys out. Boomer just headed straight for the car.

"Let's go to Taft, Polly," Janey said.

"*Taft?* Are you sure?"

"I'll show you the dayroom, Philly," Janey added.

From what Mom had said about dayrooms, I wasn't too eager to see one, but it was getting obvious that Janey wanted to show us this place.

Mom sighed. "It's your decision, Janey."

Janey had already taken off along one of the black, snaking walks.

Boomer caught up with me before I caught up with Janey. Mom trailed behind.

"This isn't so bad," Boomer said. "Right?"

"I guess not," I said. "Not yet, at least. Come on, let's stick with Janey."

I didn't notice that Mom was looking awful again until we got to Taft. It was enormous: all brick and windows. There were actually bars on the windows. The smell didn't hit us till we got upstairs into one of the long corridors. It wasn't that strong, actually, just really sickening: urine and mold and last year's sweat, but thicker, and kind of sweetened, like with one of those air freshener sprays that make me gag. Boomer and I glanced at each other, but we didn't say a thing. After all, Janey had *lived* here.

I heard Mom mutter to herself, "Same smell."

I wondered, Same as what? but we were getting to a set of double doors, and Janey had dropped behind. I turned to wait for her and my stomach cramped. She wasn't there. Not *our* Janey. I'd forgotten how she walked when she first came to our house: holding back and pushing each foot out as if the ground might disappear, and sort of looking out from under her own bowed head. I hadn't realized how much she'd changed, and now she was changing back. Maybe there really was quicksand here.

Behind her, a tall black woman in a bright yellow blouse and big gold earrings came clicking up the hall.

"I don't believe it!" she called out. "Is that Janey?"

Before Mom and Boomer could even turn around, Janey was smiling and surrounded in a hug. Then the woman held Janey at arm's length.

"You look *great,* Janey! I *told* you you could do it! Come for a visit? It's great to see you! Is this your family?"

And we were all introduced to Catherine.

"I'm a PT here—physical therapist," she explained as she led us through the double doors. "I can't get *over* you, Janey! Are you working now?"

Janey was acting more like herself. "I'm working, Catherine! I make the salads. Every morning, Catherine. I *like* making salads!"

We turned through another set of doors, and there we were in the dayroom. It was huge and sunny, with high windows down the length of it. You didn't really notice the bars. The floor was brown linoleum, and the only furniture, besides folding chairs along the walls, was a long table at the far end. A few people were sitting there doing a puzzle or something. Every time anyone spoke, there was a big echo that mixed with the hum of Catherine's voice talking quietly to Janey and Mom.

There was also a kind of tinkling, bell-like sound, and when I looked around for the reason, I saw a guy sitting cross-legged on the floor, rocking. He had pale hair, cut really short, and a pale, pale face. With both hands, he was holding a big plastic apple that made the tinkling sound as he shook it and shook it and smiled. Then he dropped it and it rolled away. He leaned and couldn't reach it. I was feeling too nervous to run over there to get it for him, when he just kind of pushed himself up on his hands and scooted over to it. I mean his legs stayed folded right up like a bow. I couldn't help it: I wanted to throw up. I went over toward the windows, where Boomer was. Maybe it was the sunlight, but Boomer looked pale, too. I squeezed his arm.

"Maybe Mom was right," he mumbled.

But Janey had started across the room, and the guy saw her. He blinked for a minute. Then his mouth dropped open into a big, drooly smile. He pushed out these two hoarse sounds that must have meant "Janey," because he said it over and over and scooted—legs still folded—so fast toward Janey that she hardly got to take two more steps. He said her name again as she sat right down in front of him, and again as he lifted his crooked arms and leaned way over his folded legs till his head touched Janey's shoulder. Janey patted his back.

"Come meet Steven," Catherine said to the rest of us, but when we all got near, he got really excited about something. He raised his arms toward Catherine and rocked forward onto his knees.

"You want to show Janey?" Catherine asked. She stretched her arms toward him, and as they held on to each other, forearms locked, Steven unfolded his legs and stood up.

"You're standing up, Stevie!" Janey said. She was still sitting on the floor, looking up at him in amazement.

"And that's not all!" said Catherine. She stepped slowly

backward, and Steven walked. His legs were still so bent I was afraid they'd crumple under him, but he was just plain beaming. I realized I was smiling, too, and the knot in my stomach had loosened a little.

"Stevie's walking, Philly!" Janey said. "He never did that, Philly!" At last I was sure she was glad we'd come.

"I told you he could, though, didn't I?" Catherine said. "They'd figured it was too late to teach him," she added to Mom. "This method isn't too good for him, actually. We're making him a special walker."

When Steven had folded himself into sitting again, he said something to Janey. It sounded like a one-word question.

"Okay, Stevie. I brought them, Stevie," Janey said, but her smile had disappeared. Her pocketbook was beside her on the floor. She opened it and took out the cards.

Steven turned his face upward toward nothing, his mouth smiling wide open. He said the one word again, and reached to take the top card as Janey placed it in his hand. Boomer and I looked at each other. We'd tried to teach Janey card games when she first came, but she never wanted to learn. I'd wondered about the reason for those cards.

Then I noticed Janey's hand was shaking. She glanced up at us, almost as if gasping for breath.

She put the cards down gently on the floor.

"I can't, Stevie," she said.

Steven still had a card and he handed it back to her, saying her name. She took it, but laid it on the floor.

"I can't play, Stevie," she said. "I have to go home now."

80

Janey stood up and hurried back across the room and out the door.

We all just straggled after her. I turned at the door and looked back. Steven had already left the scattered cards and found the apple again. He was rocking and smiling to himself.

Janey stopped halfway down the corridor and waited for us.

"She used to play cards with him," Catherine said softly. "For hours and hours on end. Just turning them over, and handing them back and forth. Janey always kept those cards in her pocket."

I hurried ahead to Janey. She turned and started walking again as I caught up. I felt kind of shy, but I put my arm around her shoulder. She looked over at me and smiled. That's when I noticed she was crying. I'd never seen Janey cry before, and it made me want to cry, too. But somehow it didn't scare me. I guess because it fit. I didn't have to wonder about the reason.

The phone was ringing when we got home: April.

"How was it? You were gone forever. I've been calling and calling."

"It was great," I said, which surprised me. I tried to explain. "I mean, it was sad and all, but I'm glad we went. I'll call you later, okay? I'm sort of tired."

"Sure, but just let me tell you. You'll never guess what I found out. June's been talking to Frank."

I really *was* tired or something. I wasn't too interested in June's latest boyfriend.

"Frank *Stapleton*," April went on, and I have to admit, I started paying attention. "He's in June's history class, remember? And he just happened to mention Danny's science-fair topic."

MARCH

10

Static electricity. Danny was right: He had a great topic. I'd read about it in the E volume. I mean, things cling or jump for no apparent reason, and it's all because of what's happening inside atoms. I had to admit, I was looking forward to seeing Danny's project.

All through February, Danny kept coming by my carrel. His grin turned into a smirk. I'd never actually known what a smirk looked like till Danny started smiling as if I was some pathetic specimen and it was cracking him up to watch me squirm. April came up with a new word: She calls Danny Stapleton my nemesis. She's probably right— I mean, a nemesis is basically someone who won't quit giving you a hard time. But now it doesn't bother me. Now that I know the reason for Danny's smirk, it kind of cracks *me* up to watch him make such a jerk of himself.

By March, I'd made it through one more hives attack and four more volumes of the encyclopedia.

In volume L, there was a picture—same as in F—of Ben Franklin with his kite, risking his life to figure out lightning. Maybe I do get obsessed about reasons, but I'm not the only one.

"Guess who," April said in her library voice.

"Hi," I said. "Any progress on your entrechat?" I knew I

wouldn't get a demonstration this time—not enough room for a fancy leap.

April took her hands from over my eyes. "Lightning, huh?"

"Yeah. Too much static electricity, and zap!: *current* electricity."

"Speaking of static, what'd he say *today*?"

"Who?"

"Your nemesis."

"Haven't seen him," I said, just now realizing how quiet the afternoon had been. "Guess he had to meet with the Nobel Prize Committee."

"I just saw him," April said. There was a funny tone in her voice, like she wasn't sure how I'd react. "He was leaving when I came in."

"Poor Danny," I said. "He's slipping."

"Well, actually . . . " April said. She dragged a chair over from the next carrel and sat straddling it, facing me, with her arms folded across the back. "You know, June's getting to know *Frank* Stapleton really well these days."

"Yeah. You told me. They're dating."

"You won't believe this, Philly."

I thought she was going to tell me June was getting married or something.

Instead she said, "I guess Danny got all upset over the weekend."

"I would've liked to see *that*."

But April looked at me closely. "No, I mean *really* upset. First he got mad about something, and then he locked himself in his room and wouldn't tell anyone what was up. But he was *crying*, Philly."

I tried to imagine Danny Stapleton crying. I tried to enjoy the idea. But it made me feel kind of sick. I always figured Danny was too much of a jerk to cry.

"Weird," I said.

"I guess Frank said it was a big deal. Their dad stood outside Danny's door for maybe half an hour before Danny let him in."

I tried to imagine a father who'd wait around just for the chance to talk to his kid—like April's dad, actually, except April wouldn't shut him out in the first place.

April caught my eye to be sure I was paying attention. "You know what he was upset about?"

I didn't have any guesses.

"The science fair," April said.

"Yeah, right."

"No, really. I guess he started way back last fall looking up about static electricity, and he got a million books, and even wrote to the science museum and all, and now he's got so much stuff he doesn't even know where to start."

"And he was *crying*?"

"A whole lot, his brother said. It was a big scene."

"Weird," I said again.

"It made me wonder," April went on, "what he'd said to you today."

"Nothing," I said. "He didn't say a thing." I was still trying to picture Danny crying.

"I just thought you'd want to know," April said. Then she leaned forward a little. "You okay, Philly?"

I guess I was looking confused. It didn't feel right feeling sorry for Danny Stapleton.

"You've got to admit," April said, "it's pretty—what's

87

that word? When you're expecting one thing and it turns out the opposite?"

"Ironic," I suggested.

"Yeah," she said. "It's pretty ironic."

On the way home, I asked April if she was staying for supper. "Mom's actually ordering Chinese," I said.

"You're kidding! She *never* gets takeout."

"We're testing for hives."

"I thought pizza was the problem."

"Yeah, but I didn't eat pizza at Dad's last time, and the hives were even worse."

"So if it's maybe Chinese, why eat it? I wouldn't mess with those hives for anything."

I had to admit, April had a point. "I have to know the reason," I said.

April shrugged. "Well, anyway, I have to get home. Dad's all worried about my math." She laughed. "He thinks he can explain it."

"Oh," I said.

I've noticed April's trouble with dividing fractions. I could probably explain it to her, but it wouldn't feel right, acting like a teacher with my best friend. I'm glad she's got a nice dad.

That night, for the first time ever, Janey knocked on my door.

Ever since we went to Morrisville, Janey seems different. Maybe it's just how I see her, because I know the reason for some things—like those cards she used to carry.

And it all fits together somehow. She seems more whole or something. But she acts that way, too, I swear—like not even being in her pj's when it was after nine o'clock.

And knocking on my door like that.

It was already open, so I just said. "Hi, Janey," trying not to act too surprised. "Come on in."

She stood just inside my room. "You can help me now, Philly," she said.

"Sure!" I said. I mean, I knew it wasn't fractions she needed help with, but I was thinking along those lines. "Help you what?"

"Call him, Philly. Now I want to."

That's when I noticed the little scrap of blue paper in her hand—the one with George G.'s address and phone number written big and clear in *my* handwriting. I felt like she was holding some huge, poisonous insect that I'd convinced her was harmless. I jumped up quickly and went to shut the door.

"Uh . . . I don't know, Janey."

"He took me in a boat, Philly. I remember. With a big white bird on the front. When I was little. Today I remembered, Philly. Kevin told me about them. Swan boats, Philly. In Boston. And I remembered. My father took me. It was fun, Philly!"

Talk about ironic. I felt sick. I'd never heard Janey say so much at once, and I was hoping she'd just keep right on going till I thought of some way out.

But now she took a deep breath, "You can help me, Philly."

She held out the slip of blue paper, and I actually

backed away from it, as if it could sting me. I sat down on my bed.

"I don't know, Janey. I mean, maybe that stuff about the boat was a *dream* or something."

"I wasn't sleeping, Philly. I was at work. Talking to Kevin. He told me about the boats, Philly. And then I remembered. Like a picture, Philly!"

This getting in touch with your past was getting out of hand. I was glad we'd gone to Morrisville, but I didn't even want to *imagine* Janey calling that jerk George G., expecting a ride on the swan boats. I was mad at myself for getting Janey thinking about this, but I was a whole lot madder at George G. This feeling of wanting to murder that guy was becoming a little too familiar. I wanted to talk to Mom. Or at least get Janey to talk to her. But there was no way I could admit to Mom how this whole big mess got started.

Janey was still standing there, looking at me and holding that nasty blue paper. I took a deep breath.

"Could you maybe sit down, Janey? I kind of need to talk to you."

Janey smiled like my talking to her was a big privilege. "Sure, Philly. I'll sit right here, Philly." And she settled into the chair at my desk.

I took a deeper breath.

"I don't think you should call him," I said. "I mean, that was a *long* time ago, those swan boats, right? And maybe he's not that nice anymore. Some fathers aren't that great, you know. Some fathers don't even deserve to be fathers. Especially for someone great like you. I mean, you *should* have a father who does nice things like that—I mean, takes you in swan boats, and talks to you when you're all upset, and maybe even helps you with your homework, but . . . "

I trailed off. Why was I talking to Janey about homework? She was sitting there with her hands in her lap, looking confused and sad.

"I'm sorry, Janey. It's just . . . I mean, what if your father's not nice?"

Janey fingered her locket.

"George G. Nicoletto," she said. "He lives in Cambridge, Philly. Like your dad. Your dad and Boomer's. Is *he* nice, Philly?"

"*Dad? Nice?*" Suddenly, I was trying to picture Dad helping me with fractions—if I needed help. I tried to picture Dad waiting outside my door while I cried—if I ever did cry. I tightened every muscle in my body, squeezing myself like a sponge to keep the anger out.

"I guess he's all right," I said.

"We could go to Cambridge," Janey said. "Together, Philly. On the bus!" She was smiling happily again.

I took a long, deep breath. "I'll tell you what," I said. "It's too late to call now, anyway—I mean, he's old, and probably goes to bed early. So let's think about it, okay? Till tomorrow at least?"

I was praying that by tomorrow I'd figure a way out.

I worried about it for half the night. I kept listening for Janey, as if she might suddenly get up and go call without me. I must have dozed a little, because I woke up suddenly, realizing something: Janey'd never called long distance.

She wouldn't know about area codes or dialing 1 or anything.

Even if she tried, she wouldn't get through to her father.

11

It was the "lamb" part of March, and warm, but Dad was still wearing that blue wool watch cap.

"So, Curly Top," he said as he unlocked the car. "Are you eating pizza these days?"

"Yeah," I said.

"Yeah," Boomer echoed as he got into the backseat. "More than her share."

I ignored him. He was just mad about missing bowling again.

"No more hives?" Dad asked me.

"Plenty of hives. Pizza or no pizza. Don't talk about it, or I'll start itching."

"So how's school?"

"Okay," I said, but I didn't mention not having a science-fair topic, or Danny Stapleton crying.

I kind of watched Dad while he drove. The evening light reflecting off the traffic made his glasses like little moving mirrors in front of his face. I was thinking about Janey's father—taking her on the swan boats once, but now not even caring if she died. Maybe once a person starts pulling away, there's no point in even *trying* to hang on. Janey hadn't mentioned George G. again, but I figured she would before long. I knew I needed to warn Mom, but I still hadn't gotten up the courage.

"How's work?" I asked Dad.

"Plenty of that, too." He flashed a smile sideways at me.

We rode in silence for a while, if there's such a thing as silence in city traffic. Dad had the heat blasting, and my neck felt hot. Maybe food wasn't even the problem. Maybe something in the *air* at Dad's was giving me hives. Finally it got too stuffy even for Dad. He turned off the blower and took off his hat. What hair he's got stood up all wispy, reaching for the ceiling. It seemed like I couldn't get away from static electricity these days, but Dad didn't seem to notice it. His hair just stayed that way till he jumped out to pick up the pizza.

When we got to his apartment and he unlocked all the locks, I was the first one through the door. I couldn't believe the smell.

"Yuck!" Boomer said, right behind me. "What *is* it?"

"Mold," I said, setting the pizza down. "I must've left an orange again." I was feeling pretty dumb for making *that* mistake twice.

Dad flicked the TV on before he even took off his jacket. His hair was still all clinging across his bald spot.

"Dad," I said. "That smell. Doesn't it *bother* you?"

He smiled. "Not particularly, I guess." He was leaning over the coffee table to drag a pizza slice onto a napkin.

"But it's *disgusting*!" I said. "And maybe *mold* could cause hives!"

I was over in the kitchen corner, trying to find the orange. It was under a pile of newspapers and a coffee-stained dish towel. As I uncovered it, the reeking cloud of mold turned my stomach right over. The orange was all green fuzz except for two tiny patches, where I managed to position my thumb and finger. I turned to chuck the thing into the wastebasket, but the wastebasket was jam-crammed and overflowing.

"Hey!" I said, looking over at Dad and Boomer.

Boomer had his headset on and his nose in the pizza. Dad was watching college basketball—live this time. He leaned back and his legs shot out in front of him on the E-Z Boy footrest.

Suddenly, I wanted to throw that moldy orange right at Dad's mussed-up head.

With my free hand, I rummaged on the counter till I found a little plastic plate—dirty, of course. I placed the orange smack in the middle, and carried it with two hands—like Janey carrying a bowl of salad—across the room. I leaned away from it, worrying about hives, but the orange didn't even roll, I was so smooth. I pulled a little tray table right in front of the TV and made a sort of pedestal with some basketball videos.

"Hey!" Dad said. "What're you doing?"

I left the orange between Dad and his game. I washed my hands at the sink, and then went to sit on the floor across from Boomer. My back was to Dad, but I could feel him watching *me* the whole time instead of basketball. I took a slice of pizza.

"Hey, Philly," Dad said, laughing a little. "What's the story?"

I guess Boomer could feel something in the room. He started paying attention. He looked at Dad, and must've noticed the orange, because then he looked quickly at me with his eyes all surprised. I knew he had a point. I'm always the one to calm Dad down, so why was I pushing things now? All I knew was I couldn't stop myself. There was something about that orange that I just wanted Dad to *notice*.

"Mold," I said, with my mouth full of sausage and black olive. "I just read about it in *M*. It's pretty interesting, actually." I swallowed. "A kind of fungus, you know, but penicillin's a mold, and—"

"Philly—" Dad started.

"Hey! Maybe it *cures* hives! Maybe I should *eat* that stuff!"

I heard Dad's chair sit up and swivel. "Come on, Philly," he said. "Get that thing out of here."

Boomer could obviously hear us over Mozart. He was staring at me, wide-eyed. I noticed he was still chewing, though.

I took another bite of pizza. "And, of course, mildew's a fungus, too. Pretty amazing stuff. Tiny little spores, but they rotted all the potatoes in Ireland, once."

"Philura," Dad said. I saw Boomer stop chewing. Dad's voice was winding up tighter. "I said, get that thing out of here. I'm your father. Do as I say."

I wanted to tell him a few things about fathers, but when I looked at Boomer, he looked like a little kid again, when he used to be scared of thunderstorms. He'd come stand in my doorway and beg with his eyes like that—as if I could protect him from lightning.

I took a deep breath and blew it out slowly.

"Sure," I said cheerfully to Dad.

As I slapped my slice of pizza back into the box and wiped my hands, something went through my mind about how even lightning can be a relief after the wrong kind of weather, but I couldn't put it into words for Boomer.

I got up and moved the tray table and took the orange, rolling dangerously, back to the kitchen corner. "Maybe I should keep this, though. It's a great specimen. I could do mold for the science fair."

Dad chuckled. "You *still* don't have a topic?"

"Nah," I said.

I poked in the trash and found a waxy bag from takeout donuts. The orange let out a last puff of stench as it hit the bottom of the bag. I was careful not to look at Dad, but I heard him sigh as he settled back in his E-Z Boy. I thought about putting the donut bag under his pillow, or in one of his slippers, or maybe in that blue watch cap. Instead, I set it on top of the trash and pushed hard till the trash smushed down and the hidden orange exploded under my hand.

"You know, Philly," Dad said, trying to smile over his shoulder, "the trouble with you is you get too full of your-self. What's the big deal about a topic? You could just flip a coin."

I really scrubbed my hands before I went back to eat more pizza. Boomer took his headset off and smiled awk-wardly. He'd even saved my whole share of pizza, like he was thanking me for shutting up.

But the pizza looked cold and greasy. I couldn't eat any

more. Maybe Dad was right. I sure was too full of something.

"Hey, Dad," Boomer piped up all of a sudden. "Let's watch that Lakers game!"

12

I didn't eat much at the Pancake Palace the next morning. It was partly that everything I looked at—the syrup, the strawberry jam—seemed to make me itch. But mostly, I just wasn't hungry. I didn't feel full, exactly—more as if I had less room inside, so it wouldn't take much to make me burst.

Boomer was bubbling with conversation all of a sudden: "Hey, Dad! Look! I never noticed this before—free side of sausage on your birthday." "Hey, Dad! Check out the haircut on that guy." "Hey, Dad! When did they knock *that* building down?"

It was fine with me if Boomer wanted to fill up the airwaves for a change. As we drove back onto residential streets, I started noticing little patches of crocus, even in front of drab old buildings. The sun was so strong through the car windows it felt like summer already.

"Hey," I said before I thought much about it, "let's do something different—like go for a ride on the swan boats. Have you ever even been on them, Dad?"

Dad smiled at me and ruffled my hair. "It's only March, Curly Top. I bet they don't run those till May at least. Want me to drop you at the library again?"

"Yeah," I said, feeling myself go even smaller inside. "In fact, let me out here. I'll walk the three blocks."

"Hey, look, Dad!" Boomer was saying as I got out. "That old car has tail fins!"

I didn't go into the library. I sat on a bench in the sun, watching other people go in. For every single one, I figured out a reason. Old, scruffy guy: can't afford his own newspaper. Nerdy high-school kid: determined to win the science fair. High-heeled, hurried woman: lost, using the pay phone.

I imagined watching myself go in. Skinny, curly-haired kid. But I couldn't think of a reason. I figured that was why I was sitting in the sun.

I went back to Dad's when the sun left the bench.

There were huge submarine sandwiches for lunch. I was picking at my turkey slices and eyeing the mayonnaise suspiciously when the phone rang.

We all jumped. Dad's phone hardly ever rings. He had to dig around for it under a heap of unfolded laundry. Boomer took off his headset.

"Hello?" Dad swallowed the food in his mouth. He was standing right in front of me. The dial part of the phone was still on the floor.

"Hi." It sure wasn't someone he was glad to hear from.

"Of course they're here. What d'you think?" Dad ran his hand over his bald spot.

"Is that Mom?" I asked, putting out my hand for the phone.

"Come on, Polly. Give me a break," Dad was saying. He sounded almost like he was begging. "This is *my* time with them."

Boomer and I looked at each other.

"I'm sorry," Dad said, sounding more annoyed. "But if it's about that girl, it'll just have to wait."

"Woman," I corrected automatically. "What *about* Janey?" I really reached for the phone this time. "Come on, Dad. Let me talk to Mom."

Dad turned his body so his back was to me and the receiver was out of reach. "No, I'm sorry," he started again, but then I could hear the edge of Mom's voice as she outtalked him. She always got supercalm and superfirm, talking to Dad.

Boomer looked at me, kind of wide-eyed again. I guess he couldn't remember too well when Mom and Dad used to argue every night at the supper table.

Dad kept shaking his head, and I could see his shoulders pulling tighter and tighter.

I stood up.

"Dad," I said. "I want to talk to Mom."

He picked up the phone from the floor and walked away from me, toward his E-Z Boy. The cord unraveled like a snake out of the laundry pile.

Then, suddenly, Dad seemed to explode. "Family!" he shouted into the phone. "Don't talk to me about family, Polly. *You* may think she's more important than their own father, but this is *my* house, and *my* time with them. So forget it!" In one angry motion, he slammed the receiver onto the phone, the phone onto the floor.

I couldn't believe it. I stood there completely frozen for a second. Dad sort of fell into his chair. He wouldn't even look at me. He stared at the blank TV screen.

101

"What's going on with Janey?" Boomer asked. I could tell he was trying not to cry.

The phone rang again. I grabbed for it, but so did Dad. He picked up the receiver and slammed it down again, then left it off the hook. I could hear the dial tone as I stood there, staring at my father, suddenly knowing that I hated him.

"I'm calling her back," I said, acting very calm and firm.

I gathered up the phone and sat down next to Boomer. I didn't dare glance at him, but I could feel him watching me and shrinking into the corner of the couch.

"Philura Mason," Dad said, his voice loud, but wobbly, "I forbid you to make that call."

As I dialed with one hand, I had to hold the phone steady with the other. I only hated Dad harder for not having push-button like the rest of the world.

"Philura Higley Mason," Dad said, standing up.

I'd only gotten through the area code, but I stood up, too. I had the phone in one hand, the receiver in the other, so when I put them behind my back, the curly cord coiled around my waist. I faced Dad.

"I am *going* to call my mother," I said.

Dad was so close, I was glaring into his eyes without even noticing his glasses.

"This is my house," he said, still sounding shaky. "I'm your father, and this is my house, and you will put that telephone down."

"I have to know about Janey," I said. I felt hot and cold at the same time, like when I get a high fever.

There was a loud three-tone beep from the telephone.

"We're sorry," chimed a nasal voice, "your call did not go through. Will you please try your call again?"

I started dialing all over. It was hard, because I was still standing up, and Dad was still right there, and my whole body was shivering.

"Listen to me, Philly." Dad tried to push the hang-up button. "I'm your *father,* do you hear?" His breath smelled of onions.

He started tugging at the phone, but I tugged back, while the nasal voice said again. "We're sorry . . . "

"Give me this phone!" Dad shouted. "I mean it, Philly! Now! I'm your *father!*" And he yanked the phone out of my hand.

"*Father!*" I yelled. "You are not! You're a jerk! A stupid, idiotic, dumb *jerk!*" I was yelling right in his face. "We *love* Janey. So there! And she loves us! *You* don't even *care* about us! You don't care about *any*thing! You're *not* a father! You don't *deserve* to be a father."

Dad's shoulders slumped. "I'm sure that's what your mother tells you," he said.

"No!" I shouted. "That's what *I'm* telling *you!* I *hate* you, do you hear? I hate you!"

"Philly," Boomer said.

Dad went to sit down, half dropping the phone onto the floor by his E-Z Boy. I still had the receiver, so the curly cord bounced between us.

I wasn't shivering anymore. I spoke slowly and carefully this time. "I hate you," I said. The phone started blaring an urgent beep, like I'd better do something or else. "I'm calling my mother," I said.

Dad didn't even look at me. "This is my house, and you will not use my phone."

I let the receiver clatter to the floor. The cord pulled it, slithering, toward Dad.

"No problem," I said. The phone kept beeping, all frantic. I went to dig my wallet out of my canvas bag. "There's a pay phone at the library."

Dad didn't try to stop me.

As I grabbed my jacket and headed for the door, Boomer looked up. He was crying silently. I wanted really badly to hug him, but I knew that would make me cry, too. I squeezed his shoulder as I passed.

"Philura," Dad said as I opened the door.

"What?"

"When you talk to that family-fun mother of yours, ask her about Aunt Philly."

"Aunt Nolly," I snapped back. "My aunt's name is Nolly." And I slammed the door behind me.

13

When I got to the library pay phone and looked in my wallet, all I had was three pennies, one nickel, and a twenty-dollar bill. Mom always gives us each a twenty when she puts us on the bus. We just give it back to her on Sunday night, but she thinks we should have money when we travel. "In case anything happens," she says.

Well, something had happened now.

The librarian at the desk didn't have change for a twenty.

"Can I borrow a dime?" I asked. "I just have to call collect."

My voice sounded shaky. I couldn't help it. She gave me the quarter and an encouraging smile.

"I'll bring it right back," I said.

The first time, the operator got a busy signal. I walked once around the lobby and tried again.

"Hello?"

"Mom!"

The operator interrupted, "I have a collect call from Flora, will you accept the charges?"

"Philura," I corrected. I must have told the operator Philura.

"I accept the charges!" Mom said. "Philly?"

"Go ahead, please!"

"Mom?"

"Thank heavens, Philly! What's going on?"

Silence.

"Philly?"

I couldn't talk. I was crying too hard. I gasped and sobbed like a baby. I guess Mom could hear me, because she just waited for a minute.

"Try to calm down, honey," she said. "Try to tell me what's going on."

"I hate him," I said. "I really hate him." I burst into sobs again.

"Where are you, Philly?"

"At the library. He wouldn't let me call you."

"Is Boomer okay?"

"Yeah," I said. "He was crying, but he's okay."

"What happened, honey?"

"Dad wouldn't let me call you. He was mad about Janey." Saying Janey's name kind of shook me awake.

"Mom, what's wrong with Janey?"

Mom gave a huge sigh. "She's gone, honey. I was out all morning. She was gone when I got back."

"*Gone?*"

"She tried to leave a note."

"But she can't write!"

"That's the problem. The note says 'Janey okay' all in capitals. Then some numbers and letters mixed up. Then 'Love Janey.' She took all her cash, and that sad old suitcase of hers, and the taxi people say they took her to the bus station, so I thought maybe she'd tried to follow you. Where else has she even *heard* about besides Cambridge?"

My stomach seemed to flop right over.

"Oh, no," I groaned.

"What's the matter, honey? Are you okay?"

"Mom," I said, but I couldn't go on.

"What is it, Philly?"

I was fumbling with the phone book that swiveled up from under the shelf. I found Nicoletto, Geo G.

"Mom? Was one of those numbers thirty-five?"

"Maybe, but—"

"'Thirty-five Winborne,'" I read.

"Philura, what are you talking about?"

"That's where he lives—George G. Nicoletto. Janey's father."

"Her *father*! What—" She stopped short. "Oh, no, Philly. Was this your doing?"

"Not exactly," I said. "Just my fault."

"You'll have to explain later," Mom said. She didn't even sound mad, which just made me scared by how worried she was. "Look," she went on, "they've already paged her at the Boston bus station, but I'll ask them to try again, and I have to call Home Care again, but then I'm driving in there, okay? It'll take me about two hours. Then we'll find Janey, Philura. We'll find her. Can you sit tight and wait for me?"

"Okay," I said. "I'll wait here—at the library."

"Does Dad know where you are?"

"Yeah, he knows, all right."

"Okay," Mom said. "I love you, Curly Top."

"Yeah," I said, trying hard not to cry again.

We said good-bye and hung up.

I collected the librarian's dime from the coin return

and started to close the phone book. Then I figured I'd memorize George G.'s address. His phone number, too, just in case.

I closed the book and let it swivel back under the shelf.

Then, as if I'd planned to all along, I picked up the phone, dropped in the dime, and dialed George G.'s number. I could pay the librarian back when Mom came.

I couldn't even imagine what I'd say. I just wished he'd hurry up and answer.

The phone rang and rang. Nobody home.

I stood there, listening to the ring and wondering if Janey could actually get there. I tried to imagine her, lugging that old cardboard suitcase, arriving on her father's doorstep. What would she do after she rang the doorbell twenty times and no one came?

I hung up, retrieved the dime, and opened the phone book again. I'd have two hours before Mom came. She wouldn't even have to know. I called a taxi.

"Thirty-five Winborne Street," I said as I got in. I tried to act like I took taxis every day. The driver didn't seem to notice me one way or the other. I watched the meter. If it got up close to ten dollars, I'd ask him to turn around and take me back.

At eight dollars and thirty cents, the driver pulled over.

"Here you are, young lady. That right there's thirty-five." He pointed beyond the passenger window to an old gray apartment building.

When he held out my change from the twenty, I just took the ten for me and a dime for the librarian. I'd heard Mom telling Janey about tipping taxi drivers.

"Thanks, kid!" he said, so I figured I'd done okay.

The minute I got out, I could see Janey through the glass doors of 35 Winborne Street. I was too relieved to be amazed. Inside, there were a few steps up to more doors. Janey was sitting on the bottom step. She had on her corduroy skirt. Her suitcase was there beside her.

She looked up when I came in. She'd been crying, but she smiled. "Hi, Philly!"

I smiled back and started crying. "Oh, Janey," I said, and sank down beside her.

We leaned to hug each other and Janey patted my back. She smelled of Ivory soap.

I sat up and swiped at my eyes and nose. "I'm sorry, Janey. I didn't understand about fathers. You're lucky he wasn't here. He's a jerk, Janey! Like my father. He doesn't even care about you. He doesn't even want to see you."

"That's right, Philly. 'Go away.' That's what he told me. 'Go away.'"

"You mean you *saw* him?"

"He opened the door, Philly." She pointed up the steps. "That one. He was old, Philly. He wasn't nice."

I tried to imagine some wrinkly guy with a gray bushy mustache coming to the door and seeing his daughter for the first time since he dumped her at Morrisville.

"Did he know it was you? Are you sure it was him?"

Janey stood up and pointed to a row of buzzers. She went over close and touched one of the names, all in capitals.

"Nicoletto," she said. "That's *my* name, Philly. I pushed the button, Philly. Then he came. I showed him my lock-et, Philly."

Janey opened her other hand, and there, sticking to her

palm, was the open heart, all tangled in its chain. George G. was still laughing.

"He's a jerk," I said. I felt like ringing his buzzer and telling him myself.

But Janey said then, "He went away. Outside. He didn't wear a coat, Philly."

"Hope it rains," I said. "And freezes. Come on. Let's get out of here." I started to get up, but then I sat down on the step again and looked up at Janey, still standing there. "How'd you get here?" I asked.

Suddenly Janey glowed with pride. She stuffed George G. into her skirt pocket and spread out her hand, touching one finger for each accomplishment.

"First I took a taxi. To the bus station, Philly. In Hampton. Then I got a ticket. 'One ticket. To Boston. Round-trip.' That's what I said, Philly. Like Polly. Then I got on the bus. Like you and Boomer, Philly." She let her hands drop. "That was a long ride, Philly!"

She sat down next to me again, as if realizing how tired she was.

"But how'd you get *here*?" I prompted.

Janey fished in her other pocket and brought out that little scrap of blue paper with my stupid handwriting on it.

"I saw taxis, Philly. Lots of them. All in a line, Philly. I showed him this."

"You're amazing, Janey," I said, and from the way she smiled, I knew she thought so, too. "Come on," I said, standing up. "Let's go home."

Janey stood up, but hesitated. "There's no phone, Philly."

Then I realized why she'd been sitting there.

"The city's different," I explained. They're so many taxis, you don't have to call—you just go out on the street and watch for one."

I'd never hailed a taxi before, but I figured it wouldn't take half as much courage as all that Janey'd just done.

I held open the door of 35 Winborne Street, and as Janey passed me, carrying that old suitcase, I actually sighed with relief.

"Or maybe we'll find a pay phone," I added.

"A pay phone," Janey said, sounding proud again. "I can use a pay phone, Philly!"

But it turned out we didn't need one.

When we got to the library, the first thing I did was give the librarian her dime.

"Sorry," I said. "I had to take a little detour."

"Are you Philly Mason?" she asked. I guess she could tell by my look of surprise that I was. "Your brother was here looking for you. He left a note."

"Thanks," I said, taking the folded paper. "Thanks a lot."

I turned away a little to read it:

> Dear Philly, Where Are You??? Dad's OK now. He's sorry. Really. Did you find out about Janey? The phone's back on the hook. You can call. I'll be the one to answer—I promise.
>
> Boomer

Janey and I both had to use the bathroom, and then she got settled into a comfy chair in the periodical room to look at a magazine. She always sits forward and lays the magazine on her knees. Then she turns each page carefully, as if it might break, starting with the back cover.

"I have to go call Boomer," I said. "I'll only be a second."

I'd gone about three steps when I realized I'd given the taxi driver my whole ten. I was down to the three pennies and the nickel.

Janey didn't have a cent in change. She'd probably just handed people tens until they said it was enough.

I thought the librarian might be getting kind of tired of my face, but she smiled when she saw me coming.

"Everything okay?" she asked. I guess it was kind of obvious that something a little weird was going on.

"Yeah. Thanks," I said. "But could I just borrow that dime a little longer?"

Boomer answered on the first ring. I told him about Janey and about Mom coming. I told him we'd be by to get my stuff, and him, too, if he wanted. Then we both kind of waited there on the phone for a second.

"You okay, Boom?" I asked.

"Yeah. You?"

"Sure," I said.

"Okay, Philly. Bye. See you."

"See you, Boom."

It wasn't much longer till Mom came. The librarian must have directed her to the periodical room, because all of a sudden Mom and Janey and I were all hugging each other and crying, and Mom was trying to get some of the story. Then I asked her for a dime and left her talking to Janey for a minute.

"Thanks," the librarian said when I gave her the dime. "But there was no rush. I see you here pretty often, don't I?"

"Yeah," I said. "Third weekend of every month. But I won't be coming back."

Mom and Janey waited in the car while I ran up to Dad's apartment to get my stuff. Boomer met me at the door with my canvas bag. All I could see of Dad was his back. He was sitting in his E-Z Boy, hunched forward. The TV wasn't even on.

"You coming?" I asked Boomer.

He glanced back at Dad. "That's okay," he said, and looked at his own hand on the doorknob.

"Sure," I said. "See you tomorrow. Same old five-forty?"

Then Boomer looked at me and smiled. "Get Mom to meet it on time for once."

Before I turned away, I reached out and mussed up his hair.

"Cut it out," he said, but he was still smiling.

APRIL

14

I'd put away the *N-O* encyclopedia without even opening it. I was just sitting at my carrel, waiting for April. She didn't have a chance to sneak up on me.

"What took you so long?" I asked

She could've gotten annoyed, but she didn't.

"I saw June," she said. "We were talking."

April and her sister talk quite a lot.

"Let's get out of here," I said.

"I thought you were aiming for *P.*"

"Nah," I said, starting for the door.

April didn't really catch up to me till we stopped near the big front doors and looked out at the rain. It was April—the month, I mean—and acting like it, too.

"You've given up," she said, without having to mention the science fair.

"Not exactly. I don't *have* to do it, that's all."

I was putting on my raincoat, which is bright yellow and crinkly and smells like thick rope or something. April was putting on hers, which is smooth and blue, with a hood.

"So where're we going?" she asked.

"For a walk?" I suggested.

I could feel April look at me closely, but I concentrated on flipping the little metal clips on my raincoat.

"Philly," she said, "it's *raining*."

"I like rain," I said. "Neat stuff. I even made some once, remember?"

"Yeah, but this is *real* rain. It'll get you *wet*." She put her hood up. "And besides, you *never* go for walks."

"First time for everything," I said.

I would have explained better if I could. It's been two weeks since I blew up at Dad, and I still can't sit still. I want to run or shout or something. I know I'm not acting like me recently. April calls me "unpredictable," but the funny thing is, the way I'm acting feels *more* like me—like who I really am, I mean.

Janey's the only one who seems to understand. She's unpredictable, too. Like calling from work to say she won't be home for supper. It's not like she never called before, but before, she used to *ask*.

With me, Janey acts like we've been somewhere important, and she's glad we went together. "That was a big trip, Philly," she says. I have to admit, I wouldn't have gone there without her. If it weren't for me, Janey might never have known the truth about George G., but if it weren't for Janey, I might never have seen the truth about Dad. What Janey and I both discovered, I guess, is that the truth may be no fun, but it sure feels better than pretending. It seems like even Mom can see that, because she never got mad at me about George G.

April and I walked over to the college, where there's sort of a park, with trees and benches and all. We didn't talk much till we got there. The rain was misty and fine, and I could feel my hair kind of tightening. I imagined I looked like the trees—all glistening with droplets, so I walked tall, as if my hair was a crown.

"You don't seem too upset," April said.

"About what?"

"Anything. The science fair. Your dad."

"I hate him," I said. It still felt good to say it out loud. "He's a jerk. Like George G."

Every so often, someone would pass through the park, huddled under an umbrella, or running zigzag to avoid the puddles. But mostly, April and I were alone.

"He's still your father," she said.

"Yeah, but that was Mom's doing—long before *I* had anything to say about it."

"She must have had her reasons," April said.

I hadn't thought about that, and I didn't particularly want to.

"I hate him," I repeated. I jumped up onto a bench and put one foot on the back, raising both arms to the sky. "You hear me?" I yelled. "I *hate* him!" I couldn't believe I was yelling in the middle of Hampton, and I couldn't believe how good it felt.

April looked like she couldn't decide whether to laugh at me or be sad. She sat down on the bench—her raincoat's long enough to sit on. Mine isn't, so I squatted there beside her with my back pressed hard against the slats.

"Maybe you could talk to him," April said.

"You sound like Boomer," I said. Boomer thinks I should talk to Dad, too. Ever since I blew up at Dad, Boomer's like the guy's best buddy. They even went bowling that night. "I don't like bowling," I explained to April, "any more than basketball."

"So invite your dad to the science fair."

"I just told you. I won't be in it."

"You still could."

"Yeah," I said, "but I don't have to." I'm not very good at explaining myself, but for April, I wanted to try. "It's just that last year it was *fun*. I mean, maybe I was obsessed or whatever, but I was having *fun*. This year's different. I mean, look at Danny. All he can do these days is mope."

The rain was still light, but it was getting through to me. Some drops from my hair collected on my neck and then trickled down my spine, inside my shirt. I shivered.

April looked at me from under her blue hood.

"You could do lightning. You really got exited about that."

"That's static electricity, same as Danny."

"He's not doing lightning, though."

I just looked at her.

"June was just telling me . . . " April said.

I wasn't sure I wanted to hear this. I got up and started walking again. April walked beside me and told me about Danny's science-fair project. I was right: I didn't want to hear it.

"*Socks?*" I said. "You're kidding."

"Something about the wash temperature, and how hot the dryer is, and whether that makes them more staticky."

"But a *chart*? He's doing static electricity, and his whole big display's going to be a *chart*? No wonder he can't hold his head up."

I have to admit, I'm getting sick of Danny acting so glum. Even a smirk would be nice for a change.

"*Socks?*" I said again.

April laughed. "Not everyone's as brilliant as you," she said, plain and simple. I stopped, and April turned to look at me. "Well you are, you know," she added.

I didn't know what to say. I've been feeling a lot of things these days, and brilliant sure isn't one of them. After messing things up for Janey the way I did, I feel about as smart as a fungus.

But I also knew what April meant.

"Come on, Philly," she said, giving me a punch in the shoulder. "It's okay. You're just lucky."

That's sort of what I was thinking, too, because when it comes to math and stuff, I *do* have it easier than April—in fact, easier than most kids, I guess. And it wouldn't be fair to pretend I don't. I mean, I sure would feel mad if April, having a great father like she does, acted like *that* was nothing special.

"You're lucky, too," I said.

April laughed. "I know. We're both lucky!" She did a pirouette or two, and then what must have been an entrechat.

I imitated her, spinning all dizzy, and then jumping so clumsy, I landed with both feet smack in a puddle.

When I got finished laughing at myself, I looked closely at April.

"*Socks?*" I asked again. "Are you sure?"

It rained harder on the way home. April went straight on to her house, and I went in our front door, dripping wet.

Mom was in the living room, reading in her favorite chair—this deep, blue one by the scraggly fig tree. She's got free time these days—the month of April's a slow one for graphic design.

"Hi, Curly Top," she called. Then she looked up from her book. "Frizz Top, I mean! Hold it right there!" I was dripping all over the hallway. "I'll get you a towel," she said, and started up the stairs. I heard her stop in to say something to Boomer, and then she came down with the towel. She brought her big purple, towelly bathrobe, too.

"Thanks, Mom."

I changed out of my wet clothes right there by the front door. It felt cozy, wearing Mom's purple robe. I went barefoot into the kitchen and got an orange, wondering if this would be the last batch of good ones this season.

Mom only glanced at me when I sat on the couch opposite her chair. I watched her for a second. She had her legs tucked up under her, and her breezy skirt trailed to the floor. As usual, wisps of hair were falling in her face. I tried to imagine her, say, fifteen years younger, deciding to marry Dad.

"Mom?" I said, but when she looked up, I looked down.

"What, honey?" she said, kind of coaxing.

"Nothing much." The orange peel was really loose—I got it off in one piece. The orange looked tiny and naked.

"Philura," Mom said.

I took a deep breath. "Well, I was kind of wondering." I put the orange back inside the peel and closed it up again. "I mean, why'd you marry Dad?" I looked up at her. "There must have been a reason."

Mom looked away. She stared at the rain clinging to the screen outside the window. She held her book in her lap, closed over one finger to keep her place. I should have known better than to ask Mom for reasons.

"That's okay," I said, leaning forward to get up.

Mom laughed, just kind of pushing air out through her nose. She looked at me, smiling, and I leaned back again.

"You just caught me off guard, honey. I figured someday you'd ask me why I divorced your dad. I've rehearsed all *those* reasons lots of times." She laughed the breathy laugh again. "But I never rehearsed one single answer for why I married the man."

"He's such a jerk," I said. She'd heard that a few times on the way home from Cambridge.

"He's a very bright man, honey. *Extremely* bright. That's where you get it."

I'd started eating my orange, but I stopped chewing and looked at Mom. This was getting kind of repetitious, people talking about me being smart.

Now Mom really laughed.

"You act like it's news! 'Gifted' is what your teachers always call you."

I swallowed my mouthful of orange too fast, and had to work at getting it down.

"*Gifted?*" I said, sounding strangled.

"Well, I don't much care for labels—negative *or* positive—but it's what they called your father, too."

I knew Mom was trying to say something nice, but I didn't want to hear it. Admitting I was lucky was one thing, but I sure wasn't going to owe my luck to Dad.

"He can keep his gifts to himself," I muttered.

Mom didn't miss a beat. "That's exactly what he does," she said. She sighed. "I guess in college I was flattered he liked me. He was the campus 'brain,' and all that moodiness just made him seem 'deep.'" She smiled. "I'd be running around picking apple blossoms, and he'd be sitting under the tree, somberly explaining *exactly* how pollination works."

Mom looked out the window again. "But what's the point of knowing everything if you don't dare care about any of it?" She paused, but I knew she wasn't expecting an answer. "I guess I imagined I could *make* him happy— or at least that you kids would."

Mom turned to me again. "But your father's unhappiness started way back, Philura. It's not my fault or yours." I could tell she'd worked around to the rehearsed part. "He just won't move on. He won't enjoy all he's got, because he's still resentful for what he never had."

I wasn't going to fall for that unhappiness stuff.

"He's a jerk," I insisted, and stood up. "I don't care about the reasons—he's still a jerk."

When I got to the door, I turned around, holding half my orange in one hand, and the peel in the other.

"Hey, Mom," I said. "What did he mean? He told me to ask you about Aunt Philly."

I thought Mom would just correct me. My aunt's name is Nolly—Noreen. I thought Mom would just correct me, and then I'd grab my wet clothes from the hall and finish my orange upstairs. But Mom looked at me for a long, surprised moment. Then she winced and sank back as if she'd been slapped in the face.

15

I started forward. "Mom, are you okay?"

Mom had looked away, out the window. I could only see the side of her face, but it was twisted all strange. I backed away.

"Mom," I said. "I don't *have* an Aunt Philly."

Mom almost whispered. "Not anymore," she said.

I stood in the doorway. I didn't move at all. I just stood there in Mom's purple robe, filling up with questions.

"You're kidding," I said, but I could hardly hear myself. "Mom, you're kidding."

Mom shook her head, still looking away, and suddenly I didn't know her at all.

My voice came out croaky, but a little stronger. "I have an Aunt Philly? You have a *sister* named Philly?"

"Had," Mom said quietly. "*Had* a sister named Philly."

"But Mom!" I said. "An aunt? With *my* name? How come you never told me?"

Mom looked at me then. "Go call Boomer, Philura," she said, "and I'll tell you now."

Suddenly I remembered the orange in my hand, but even that looked far away. I set it down somewhere and turned toward the hall, calling Boomer in a voice I didn't recognize.

I had to go upstairs to get him because he had his headset on. "You have to come," I said. "Right away."

I must have scared him. He followed me without even asking why.

We sat on opposite ends of the couch. Boomer had the headset around his neck like some clunky piece of jewelry. He looked at Mom and then looked at me, but I couldn't even give him a clue.

Mom put her book aside and squared herself in her chair. She planted her elbows on the chair arms and folded her hands in front of her, as if buckling a seat belt.

"Your aunt Noreen and I . . . ," she started. She swallowed very carefully. "We had an older sister who died." I could feel Boomer glance at me again, but he didn't interrupt, and Mom went on. "When we were little, we had a big sister named Philura."

I looked up sharply. "You said I was named after your great-grandmother."

"So was she," Mom said.

"But—what. . .?" Boomer sputtered.

I felt the same way: too many questions to put into words.

Mom just kept going. "The hard thing was, she had Down's syndrome."

I sat forward suddenly. "Down's syndrome?" But it still took a second to sink in. Mom had had a sister with mental retardation. A different kind from Janey's, but mental retardation. "Janey," I said, not making much sense. "Mom! Janey!"

I wanted to stop Mom now. I wanted to shake her. I could have known this all along.

126

But Mom seemed determined to keep going. "I didn't realize at the time, of course—I was only five when—" Mom froze for a second, the way Janey used to, except Mom swallowed hard a few times. Then she started again. "I was too little to know how unusual it was, keeping Philly at home. She was just my big sister to me. She was nine years older, and she liked to rock me on her lap. I adored her, I remember that—the way she smiled, crinkles all over her face."

"Mom," Boomer said. He sounded all concerned, but I wasn't about to feel sorry for Mom.

"You could have told me," I said.

Mom seemed far away, as if she'd forgotten we were there.

I reminded her. "When did she die?" I asked.

Boomer gave me a shocked look.

Mom just answered my question. "When I was nine and she was eighteen. She got hepatitis in the institution, and she died."

"I thought—" I started.

"But you said—" Boomer was saying.

Mom got up and walked to the window. She picked a few dead leaves off the fig tree.

"Something must've finally convinced my parents. Better for her. Better for the other kids. Better for everyone. People really believed that back then." Mom took a very deep breath. "I was only five, but I still remember leaving her there."

"You mean you took her to Morrisville?" Boomer asked.

Mom seemed to remember she was talking to us. She turned and looked straight at Boomer. "I grew up in Ohio, remember? Bentley, the place was called. But it was just like Morrisville."

"Wow," Boomer said.

"Except," Mom added, "there was a merry-go-round."

"A *what?*" I couldn't believe any of this was real.

Mom went back to her chair.

"I know it sounds incredible, but there really was. Some rich guy's idea of a kindly donation. A whole separate building. An indoor merry-go-round. That's how they got Philly to let us leave her."

Mom paused, and Boomer and I waited.

"When we went for visits, she was always in her sickly smelling ward, or that noisy dayroom. But I kept imagining her riding that foolish merry-go-round, smiling all crinkled at us."

Mom's voice was cracking. It was getting hard to stay angry at her.

"Mom," I said, and she just plain burst into tears.

Boomer fingered his headset like he was dying to put it back on.

I just sat there, staring at my hands. I tried to imagine an aunt who looked like Mom and Aunt Nolly, and smiled like Janey's friend Kevin. An aunt whose name was Philura.

"I'm sorry, kids," Mom said, and she got control of her tears.

"Why didn't you tell us?" I asked again.

"It was just hard," Mom said limply. "I didn't want to think about it. I wanted to move on."

I guess moving on felt like a suggestion, because we all just got up at once.

Mom was giving Boomer a hug when I went into the hallway to get my clothes. She followed me and hugged me, too. Maybe it was the wet clothes I was holding between us, but even with Mom's arms tight around me like that, I felt a million miles apart.

16

It was Thursday, so April had gymnastics. I'd already been for a walk, and I didn't have anything to do at the library, but I sure wasn't going to go home. Whenever I'm around Mom, I get mad. I get mad if she's silent, because there's something she's not telling. I get mad if she talks, because everything she tells me—about Aunt Philly, about Dad— she could have told me all along. I mean, when I was looking for the reason for rain, if the librarian had hidden all the books that explained it, I would have wanted to *kill* her.

If Mom had told me about Aunt Philly, I would've known all along how Janey fits. She's like my aunt *would* have been: part of the family, but kind of separate, too.

And if Mom had talked to me about Dad, I would've known all along what a jerk I've got for a father. I wouldn't have had to spend the third weekend of every month figuring it out for myself.

When I got to the library, I headed for the encyclopedias out of habit. That's when I saw Danny Stapleton. He was at the far end of the big room I call the banquet room, just getting up from the table where he'd been working. He slumped off toward the bathroom or somewhere without noticing me—or anything else, probably. He was too busy feeling sorry for himself.

Suddenly I'd had it with Danny, too. He's really smart, and he knows it, and it just made me *mad*, his making static electricity boring.

I grabbed the *L* volume and found the right page on my way to Danny's table. I didn't even care if other people noticed. His notebook lay open to pages all covered with squiggles and doodles, which just made me madder. I laid the encyclopedia on top, open to this two-page, full-color, glossy photo of lightning over the desert. Those big saguaro cacti looked like silhouettes of fat-armed dancers, and the lightning went all across the sky. Even Danny would have to notice it looked a whole lot more interesting than socks.

I went back for the *P* encyclopedia, which was where I'd left off, and headed for my carrel.

Once I started reading, I couldn't help it: I got interested in things. Like the reason for pain. It's amazing. I mean, why do we have "more nerve endings for pain than for any other sensation"? And how come "even with the same stimulus, some individuals feel more pain than others"?

"Some pain," the encyclopedia said, "is caused by mental disturbance, with no nerve endings affected." So what makes it hurt? I was wondering.

I guess I got so involved, I didn't hear the untied hightops coming.

"Hello, Philura."

I have to admit, it was good to see Danny grin for a change. He puffed up and tried to look down his nose. He was full of himself again.

"Why, hello, Daniel."

131

Calling him Daniel just makes him grin bigger.

"Still looking for a topic, Philura?"

I figured I might as well play it straight.

"I decided not to enter the science fair, Danny." Then I couldn't help adding, "Thought I'd give someone else a chance. There *might* even be hope for you!"

"Oh, I've got a winner, all right! This great idea just *struck* me."

I figured I'd let him crack himself up, but it was hard to keep a straight face.

"Great," I said. "Hope you knock the judges' socks off!"

Danny didn't even flinch.

"Oh, I will, Philura. I will. If I don't get too much static from my teammate."

The static was expected, but the teammate thing wasn't. I knew some kids did the science fair in pairs, but I couldn't imagine Danny thinking anyone was half smart enough to work with his high-and-mighty self. And I couldn't imagine anyone who *was* half smart enough agreeing to work with Danny.

I glanced at Danny, still lost for a snappy comeback. He glanced away. Then we both looked at each other. Right there as I watched, Danny's grin changed. The mocking part drained away. He still looked very pleased with himself, but also a little embarrassed. Danny was actually smiling.

"You're kidding," I said.

"Well, you know—one good turn . . . "

"How'd you know it was me?"

Danny actually laughed. "Come on. I'm not *that* dumb."

"Oh."

"So." He paused. "Display ideas." He paused again. "There's the one where you make puffed rice jump around. . . ."

"Puffed rice?" I hadn't read that one. "Oh, yeah," I said, pretending I had.

"And maybe that picture blown up like a poster, or—"

"And there'd have to be a lightning chamber," I interrupted. "All dark, so people could see the sparks. But before that—" I caught myself and bit my lip.

"So are you in?" Danny asked.

"Sure," I said, without stopping to think.

Danny kind of shuffled in place.

"We can start tomorrow," I said, because there were things in volume *P* I still wanted to read.

"Anything you say, Philura, but . . . " Danny was grinning like his old self again, which means like a jerk, I guess. I was having second thoughts. "There's only one problem," Danny said.

"Only one?"

"When we win—which we definitely will—who gets to keep the blue ribbon?"

17

The third Friday in April was all sun and blossoming trees. The bus station seemed dark and stuffy, so while Mom was buying Boomer's ticket, I waited outside on the bench. I have to admit, I couldn't sit still. I was wishing Janey was there to talk to, but Janey was off with friends again.

After a while, Boomer came out and sat down next to me in the sun. He didn't have his headset on, and he wasn't sulking. So why couldn't he have been like that before? He did still have his clothes in a lumpy paper bag, and he put it between his feet. We were silent for a minute. Then we glanced at each other.

"Going bowling again?" I asked.

Boomer grinned sideways at me, embarrassed. "I guess so."

"Great," I said, only a little sarcastic. It seemed like everybody could change once it didn't do *me* any good.

Boomer mumbled so low, I could hardly understand him, "You could come, too, Phil."

"I don't like bowling—wearing somebody else's sweaty shoes, and—"

"Come on, Philly. You know what I mean."

"You want me to miss April's birthday party?"

"She would've changed it—she did last year."

"But she didn't this year."

Boomer lifted the paper bag onto his knees and got out his tape player. I leaned back and closed my eyes in the sun, but I could hear him switching the tape.

"Are you *ever* coming back?" he asked.

I opened my eyes enough to look at him sideways. He was squinting at me, worried. I had to admit: We'd always done this together. It felt awful weird, both facing the weekend alone with one parent.

I sat up. "Don't worry, Boom!" I slapped him on the back. "It'll be great! Now you'll *always* get the window seat!"

Boomer didn't smile. "He was really upset, Philly. *Really*, I mean."

"Yeah, right," I said. "Come on, Boom. Don't worry. Just slip in the right video. He'll be back to his old self in no time."

"He *said* he was sorry," Boomer muttered.

I could tell this was hard for him, so I didn't laugh.

"Yeah," I said. "He told *you* to tell me." I folded my arms and squeezed them against me. "And I've just been *swamped* with cards and flowers."

"Dad's not *like* that," Boomer said, really forceful. It made me look at him. He had a point.

"Yeah," I said. "I noticed."

Boomer put on his headset and started adjusting the volume. I pulled one side away from his ear.

"Look at it this way," I said. "All the more pizza for you!"

Boomer's smile was still tight. "I'll probably get hives," he said.

I sat back and closed my eyes again. The sun made a red swirly curtain on the back of my eyelids. I watched it for a second without knowing I was thinking.

Suddenly, I sat up and looked at Boomer. "Hey!" I said. "*Hey!*" I shook Boomer's shoulder. "It's April! Hey, Boom! It's *April!*"

Boomer took his headset off and held it in his lap. He looked at me like I was crazy. "What about her?"

"No, I mean it's almost *May!*" I was checking in my pockets for my little date book. I couldn't remember bringing it with me—not for a long time, actually. But I couldn't remember deciding *not* to bring it, either. "It's almost May, Boomer, and no hives! Not this month, not last month—not since *February!*"

I jumped up to run inside, but I nearly crashed into Mom coming out to find us. "Hey, Mom! Guess what! No hives!" I turned around a few times with my arms in the air and a big grin on my face.

Mom smiled at me. "Congratulations, honey," she said, but she didn't sound surprised. I had the funny feeling my news wasn't news to Mom, which made me remember I was mad at her.

I stopped twirling. "But I ate everything the same."

Mom smiled. "But just think what else is new since February."

"Besides my blowing up at Dad, you mean?"

Mom looked right over my head at the parking lot.

I followed her gaze, but couldn't see what had distracted her. When I glanced back at her face, I realized she was trying not to smile.

"Mom?"

She looked at me then. "*Besides* blowing up at Dad?" she said.

Then it hit me. "Oh. You mean . . . ?" Suddenly I felt incredibly dumb. "You mean it wasn't even allergies, you think."

Now Mom smiled. "Not to food, at least." She ruffled my hair and turned to Boomer. "Come on, Boom. Your bus is loading."

Boomer sat on the side where we could see him. I have to admit, his face looked awfully small in the wide window of that huge, broad-sided bus. He grinned and waved, and I grinned and waved back, but when our eyes actually met, I had to look away and swallow hard. I wished the bus would hurry up and leave, but then when it did, I wished it was still there so I could still see Boomer, and not be feeling hollow like I was.

Mom and I were silent most of the way home. I kept thinking about the hives. The doctor'd mentioned "possible emotional causes," but it just hadn't sounded like me. Still, if pain could be "caused by mental disturbance with no nerve endings affected," why not hives?

"Did you already call the doctor?" I asked Mom, and she nodded, knowing what I meant.

"What'd you tell her?"

Mom smiled. "I told her you'd found your own way around those hives."

I smiled back. "Yeah," I said. "And I did it without knowing the reason."

MAY

18

"Hey, Danny," I said in my library voice. "Look at this."

We were across from each other at a table in the banquet room. There were books spread out between us, and one of them was *The Great Mysteries of Science*. It said that even the experts don't really *know* how static electricity works.

"'Our information is still based largely on theory,'" I read to Danny.

Danny took the book and shut it decisively.

"But we have to *explain* it," he said. "It's *May*, Philura. We have to *focus*."

"Okay, okay," I said. With only ten days to the science fair, he did have a point.

Danny grinned. "Now, if you're having trouble understanding, Philura—"

"Go fly a kite," I said.

Just because we're working together, it doesn't make Danny easy to get along with. He forgets a lot that we're on the same team.

"A kite?" he said. "That would be unwise. Ben Franklin—"

"Ben Franklin was great," I said. Sometimes if I play it straight, Danny forgets his jerk routine.

"Yeah, my mom named my brother after him," he said.

"Ben? How old's Ben? I've only heard about Frank."

"Yeah. Frank. Franklin. That's his name."

"Franklin? Oh, yeah. Neat. I mean, at least if his name's a little strange, he knows the reason. Not like *my* mom—" I stopped myself. I guess I'd gotten used to Danny using my real name, but that didn't mean I could trust him.

Anyway, Danny had his nose in a book all of a sudden.

"So," I said. "Who'd she name *you* after? Daniel Boone? Daniel Webster?"

Danny glanced up just long enough to look offended. "My mom's a *scientist*," he said, as if I should already know.

"She is? Really?"

Danny was kind of mumbling. "Yeah. A professor. At the college."

I'd have to think about that—it might explain some things about Danny. But I was concentrating on names. "A famous scientist named Daniel," I wondered aloud, but I couldn't think of a single one. "I give up. Who?"

Danny looked up and caught my eye for a second. "Promise you won't tell?"

I couldn't believe it. Danny Stapleton was going to tell me a secret. I looked straight back at him. "Promise."

"The guy who did all the evolution stuff. Why giraffes have long necks."

"You mean Darwin? How we came from the apes? He was *really* big on reasons. He was great!" Then I realized: "But, Danny—Darwin's name was Charles."

"Yeah. And Franklin's name was Ben."

I looked at him. I could feel a smile creep onto my face. Danny looked away, but he was smiling, too.

"You mean to say," I said, sticking my hand out across the table, "I'm entering the science fair with Mr. *Darwin* Stapleton?"

I was using my library voice, and there wasn't anyone nearby, but Danny still glanced around as if someone might hear.

"Yeah," he said, but he didn't shake my hand.

"How'd you do it? Keep your real name a secret, I mean. *I* sure never could."

"My dad let me—when we moved. Filled out all the forms with just Danny. My real name's probably in the records somewhere, but most people just assume it's Daniel."

"Like I did."

Danny was grinning again. "Yeah." He looked at me, and I knew what was coming. "So where'd you get a name like Philura?"

I took a deep breath. "My great-grandmother. And my aunt. They were both Philura Higley, so Higley's my middle name, if you can believe that, but I kind of like my name now, because my aunt was really neat."

I stopped to take a breath, and there was a little extra silence—just enough for panic to slip in. Why was I saying all this to Danny? *He* hadn't promised not to tell.

I straightened some papers in front of me. "Say, Danny—"

"I know, I know," he interrupted. "It's all a secret, right?"

I'd already started nodding before I said, "No. Actually, it's not." Suddenly, I sat up tall, almost puffed up like Danny. "I'm Philura Higley Mason—and I've got a good reason to be."

"Now, about this lightning," Danny said.

"Right." I put my hands up like blinders. "Focus."

"Unless you're too tired, Philura. We don't want to strain your brain."

"Go fly a kite, Darwin Stapleton."

The minute I got home, I went straight back to Mom's studio. She's crazy busy again, but I didn't much care. I just plopped right down in the canvas chair.

"Why?" I said. "*Why* was it such a big secret?"

Mom swiveled around on her drafting stool. She looked a little startled, but a lot amused.

"Hi, Curly Top!" she said. "How was your day? Mine was quite fine, thank you."

She had a point.

"Hi," I said.

"Is this Aunt Philly on your mind?"

"Yeah," I said, trying to warm up my anger. "Why was she such a big secret? It's like we're supposed to be *ashamed* of her or something."

"Oh, honey," Mom said, "I wasn't ashamed of Philura." She paused and put her pencil behind her ear. "I guess I just felt guilty. Because that was the thing then, you know—that we 'normal' kids deserved a 'normal' home. So it felt like my fault that they took her to Bentley. It felt like my fault that she died."

"You still could have told me," I muttered.

Mom sighed. "I guess that's the trouble with secrets—the longer you keep them, the harder they are to tell."

I tried to find my anger, but it was gone. Mom wasn't apologizing; she wasn't even looking for sympathy. She was just explaining her reasons.

"I could have known all along," I said.

"I know, honey." She shrugged. "What can I say? I'm not a perfect parent—far from it." She waited till she caught my eye. "But an imperfect parent can still love you, you know."

"I know, Mom," I said, because it was true: Even being mad at Mom, I'd always been sure she loved me.

"I've made lots of mistakes in my life, Curly Top."

"Like marrying Dad?"

Mom laughed this really sad laugh and looked at her hands for a minute. Then she looked up at me.

"That's one mistake I'm glad I made. For two very good reasons."

"Reasons?" It wasn't a word Mom used a lot.

"You and Boomer," Mom answered, smiling. "If it weren't for Dad being your father, you kids wouldn't be you."

I didn't want to hear about Dad's "gifts" again, but I didn't have to worry. Mom had turned back to her work. She can never talk long about Dad. Too busy moving on, I thought, feeling my anger stir. That's probably just what George G. Nicoletto had done: moved on. I looked at the wisps of Mom's hair floating in all directions around her head. An imperfect parent can still love you, I repeated to myself. George G. just got so imperfect he wasn't a parent at all anymore.

Was Dad *that* imperfect?

I thought about it for quite a long time, and I had to admit: Even being mad at Dad, I still wasn't sure he *didn't* love me.

The weekend after the science fair would be the third weekend in May. A Dad weekend. And maybe the swan boats would be running.

I stood up.

"What's for supper?" I asked Mom.

"I think Janey's making it."

"Tofu-cheese squares? Boomer will be thrilled." Boomer hates the *idea* of tofu.

"I think he's in there helping," Mom said.

"Yeah. Probably adding peanut butter and ketchup."

As I left the studio, Mom called after me, "How's the lightning project?"

"Great," I called back. "We're going to shock you!"

19

On Saturday, I spent the afternoon at Danny's so we could make the lightning chamber and get together all the other stuff we'll need. His dad helped. His dad's this funny little shy guy, sort of pudgy and sweet, who made little suggestions, and fixed us lemonade, because it was actually hot.

Even on a Saturday, Danny's mom was over at the college. He said he doesn't see her that much. "She's real busy," he explained, not looking at me.

A *lot* of parents are imperfect, I guess.

We were in Danny's garage, just finishing tacking black cloth to a wooden frame, when Mr. Stapleton came out to tell us what they were saying on the radio: record temperatures for May, and even thunderstorms predicted.

"Lightning," he said, smiling at us. "A good omen, I'm sure."

The lightning didn't come till evening.

Mom had taken Boomer to a chamber music concert, leaving Janey and me with the supper dishes. I didn't mind. I hadn't really talked to Janey in a long time, and I still hadn't apologized for stirring things up about George G.

"I'll dry, Philly," Janey said.

We had the back door open to let in the breeze, and as we both cleared and scraped and stacked, I told Janey about the lightning chamber and the lemonade. Then I asked her about work and her friend Kevin. She said he's got a job now, bagging groceries at the Save-Mart.

"He puts things in the bags, Philly. Cans on the bottom, eggs on the top. And he talks to people. Kevin likes talking to people, Philly. And he gets a paycheck! Not in the mail like my check, Philly. Mr. Watroba gives it to him. Every Saturday!"

I didn't look at Janey. I watched the suds grow into a puffy mound as the water filled the sink. I was wondering when Janey'd get a job and a real paycheck. And then her own apartment.

"You know what?" I said.

"What, Philly?"

Janey stood there with the dish towel, waiting for the glasses I was washing.

"It's May, Janey. That means a year since you moved in."

"A year, Philly?"

Janey looked out the window for a minute, trying, same as I was, to understand the meaning of a year. The sky had darkened, and the breeze was becoming a wind, tossing the lilacs in the neighbor's yard and bringing their smell through the screen door to us. Janey had lived with us a whole year. *Only* a year. And now I couldn't imagine our family without her.

"You're real different, you know," I said.

Janey was drying a glass as carefully as if it were fancy crystal. "No, Philly. I'm still Janey."

"I know. But I mean—you've learned so much. What if . . . ?" I cleared my throat and made my voice sound extra cheerful. "Pretty soon, I bet, you're going to leave. Leave us and get your own apartment."

"My own apartment? You think so, Philly?"

I had to smile back at her. "For sure, Janey. You're amazing!"

We worked in silence for a while. Then there was a rumble from the thickening sky. Janey went to look out the door. "That's thunder, Philly."

"They said we'd have a storm. Great!"

I left the sink, drying my hands on Janey's towel as we went out onto the back stoop.

The wind had calmed. Everything waited. I stood next to Janey and waited, too.

Then there was lightning—distant, but so sudden we both jumped. It was sharp lightning, the kind that you see like a big crack in the sky. And before the rolling thunder reached us, there was another flash, and another.

"Oh!" Janey said. She turned to go inside, and I followed.

With the screen door closed safely behind us, we stayed in the doorway, hoping to be startled again.

But the lightning quickly faded into the distance, dragging the thunder with it. Janey sighed and seemed to remember the dish towel in her hand. She looked at the plates in the drainer and the pots and pans still to be washed.

"We'll do the rest, Philly," she said. "Then you can help me."

"Help you?" Every time Janey says that, I still think of her wanting to call George G. "Sure," I said. "Do what?"

"Write his address, Philly. I already put the stamp on. In the corner, Philly."

I plunged a saucepan into the sink and swished a copper scrubbie around in it. "You're writing him?"

"I bought a card, Philly. With flowers on it. He likes flowers, Philly." Janey had put down the dish towel and was reaching with both hands to put a plate away.

I tried to imagine George G. liking flowers. "You're sending him a card?" I was careful not to sound too surprised. "I mean, I just wondered why."

"I miss him, Philly. I'm going to visit again. Rich said so. He'll take me, Philly."

The pan was clean, but I kept on swishing at it while Janey dried another plate. I'd always thought Janey's caseworker was right about not cutting off the past, and after all, *I'd* decided to go visit *my* father again. But all I could think of was Janey on the steps of 35 Winborne, clutching that cardboard suitcase. As I put the pan in the drainer, I turned to face Janey.

"Let me get this straight," I said. "You mean Rich is taking you to visit your father?"

Janey froze the way she used to. When she jerked back to life, she almost dropped the plate.

"Not my father, Philly. No, Philly. Not my father. He wasn't nice, Philly. Remember? He told me to go away. Remember, Philly?"

"Yeah. I remember."

Janey paused to put the plate away. Then she turned to me. "My father's a *jerk*, Philly."

I almost smiled. "I know what you mean," I said. I grabbed the next pan. "But, so who's the card for?"

"Stevie, Philly. My friend. Remember? At Morrisville? I miss him, Philly. You can help me."

"Oh, right. Of course." I could never forget Steven. "I don't know his address, but, sure."

I knew Janey wouldn't even know his last name, but I'd figure something out. I mean, there's only one state school in Morrisville. And probably only one Steven still left there. I should have guessed: No matter what, Janey would find a way to keep in touch with Steven.

"Hey," I said. "When you get your own apartment, I bet you'll even keep in touch with *me*!"

Janey finished nesting a plate safely on the stack, then turned to me, looking too surprised to smile. "Of course, Philly! I *always* will! You're my family, Philly!"

"Okay, okay," I said, laughing. "I get it." I'm still not sure I know *why* Janey fits, but I certainly know she does.

I waited a moment before I said, "You don't wear your locket anymore, do you?"

Janey set a plate back in the drainer and put her hand to her throat. "I still have it, Philly. In my room. He used to be nice, Philly."

We both swished and swiped again, letting the sadness settle.

"I'm sorry, Janey," I said. "About your father, I mean. I didn't know. I didn't mean to make you sad."

There was that look of surprise again. It seemed like Janey was having trouble believing how slow I was to catch on.

"But I'm happy, Philly! I can take the bus now. I *know* I

can. I'm going there, Philly. With Kevin. We can ride on the swan boats!"

Janey does seem glad for that awful day in Cambridge, and I have to admit, I'm glad too. It's not like it's fun, realizing what a jerk my father can be, but it's easier, somehow, not expecting him to be someone else.

"That's what I like about you, Janey," I said.

She smiled broadly. "I like you, too, Philly."

"Yeah, but I mean, you're amazing. It's like you can keep your past without getting stuck there." I paused, trying to find the right words. "And you don't have to throw it all away just to keep moving." I knew Janey didn't understand what I was saying. I wasn't even sure *I* did. But the thing about Janey is, she doesn't *have* to stop and understand everything before she can take the next step.

"I want to be like that," I said. "I want to be like you, Janey."

Janey froze, dish towel wadded inside a saucepan. But she wasn't thinking. She was looking straight at me, her eyes deep and wide. "Oh, no, Philly. You stay like you are! You're smart, Philly. You can explain things. Like reasons, Philly. And that lightning."

I had to laugh. "Reasons aren't everything," I said.

And it really does seem, now, that in some way, Janey understands a lot of things—maybe even lightning—better than I do. Because if you *think* you can understand lightning, and you "focus," like Danny says—on atoms, and the negative and positive charges, and all—you can just forget to notice what lightning's really like: huge and scary and beautiful—and maybe impossible to understand.

Which is how Janey sees it, I bet.

*   *   *

The rain never came.

When the dishes were done and Janey had wiped every crumb from the counters and pushed the chairs in neatly at the table, she stood and looked around with satisfaction.

"You can help me now, Philly," she said.

Steven's card was huge and flowery, and across the front, in big gold letters, it read CONGRATULATIONS ON YOUR RETIREMENT!

"Janey," I started, but I stopped myself.

Just knowing the card was from Janey, Steven would get the right message.

We walked the few blocks to the nearest mailbox. The sky overhead was still low and heavy, but the sun was on the horizon. The light had to sneak under the clouds, so it seemed to shine *through* everything, and the dandelion puffs in the vacant lot glowed like tiny magic wands.

I watched Janey open the mailbox, set the card gently on the little horizontal door, then close the door so carefully it didn't make a sound.

153

20

The Regional Elementary Science Fair is held in the high-school gym. Danny and I had booth thirty-one.

Danny's dad dropped us there after school, and we spent all afternoon setting up: not just the dark chamber for the sparks, but all the balloons, and puffed rice, and the models of atoms to show the reasons for it all.

I'd made a sign for our table:

> THE REASON FOR LIGHTNING
> Learn about Static Electricity
> and Shock Yourself!
> by
> Danny Stapleton
> and
> Philura Higley Mason

The fair didn't start till seven, so Mom picked us up to take us out for pizza.

Janey was in the front seat, Boomer in the back. I made a big deal of holding the door open for Danny. I bowed and swept the air with my arm. "Beauty before brains!" I was cracking myself up.

Then as I climbed in after him, and Mom and Boomer

were saying hi, I realized I hadn't told Danny about Janey.

"Uh, Danny," I said. "This is Janey. I mean, I guess, TJ—right, Janey? TJ Nicoletto."

Janey twisted in her seat and stuck her hand over her shoulder. She smiled really big.

"You're Danny," she said. "Danny Stapleton. Philly's friend."

Danny shook Janey's hand without even glancing at me. "Hi," he said.

And he didn't act like a jerk the whole time at Pizza Paradise.

I figured when we got back to the gym, he'd ask me about Janey, but all he said was, "Is she like your aunt or something?"

"Yeah," I said, "a *lot* like my aunt," and I had to smile. I guess when something really fits, nobody much wonders about the reasons.

Danny and I checked everything, and then stood there with our feet a little apart and our hands behind our backs—like the pictures I'd seen of soldiers "at ease." But the soldiers looked stiff as boards, and we weren't exactly relaxed.

Danny took a walk around to see the other displays, and I did the same when he got back. A lot of kids had worked on ecology and all: which trash rots best, and how to use solar energy.

"Important stuff," I muttered sideways to Danny, once we were standing at ease again. "Everybody else did stuff that really matters."

"Yeah," he said, "but ours is more fun."

Then our first "customers" showed up—somebody else's parents, probably—and Danny and I were so glad to have something to do, we were stumbling all over each other handing them balloons and pieces of wool cloth. They drifted off without even trying the lightning chamber.

We straightened everything and stood around some more. Then, all of a sudden, it seemed like the gym was mobbed. Danny and I were working like crazy, trying to help people make their hair stand on end, and explaining about electrons moving from here to there, and showing them how to make lightning with friction and their own fingertips. Lots of people had to take their shoes off for the lightning part, so there was sort of a sweaty smell, and there were balloons popping, and people going "Ah!" and "Cool!" and laughing, and little kids coming back for the fifteenth time.

Danny's dad came, and Frank, but I hardly got to notice, and when Janey and Mom came by, Janey laughed at the wisps of Mom's hair reaching out sideways for the balloon, and Mom got really kind of giggling, and the two of them were acting a lot like little kids as Danny escorted them to the lightning chamber. I was showing someone how to rub a comb with wool to make puffed rice jump, when I heard Janey say proudly, "Look, Polly! I did it! I made lightning, Polly!"

Things calmed down for a while. April came by with her family. Even June was with them.

"That's Frank's girlfriend," Danny whispered as they left.

I raised my eyebrows at him. "How do you think I found out about the socks?"

Then things got busier again.

I was explaining about positive and negative charges to some of Boomer's friends when I saw April kind of gliding through the spaces in the crowd. She was heading straight for me.

"So one thing's getting more and more negative," I was saying, "and the other's getting more and more positive—"

"Philly!"

"—till *zap*! there's a big flash, and everything kind of evens out again."

"Philly! Guess what!"

"And Danny, here, will show you the lightning chamber," I told the kids.

I grinned at Danny, who tried to look huffy, but was already saying, all dramatic, "Okay, kids. Prepare yourselves for a shock!"

I was still grinning when I turned to April.

"What's up?" I said.

April pointed across the gym. The crowd had thinned enough so I could see Mom standing near the door with Janey. I almost didn't recognize the guy Mom was talking to. Maybe because he wasn't wearing his blue wool watch cap.

I just looked at Dad standing there. People passed between us, but I just blinked and looked at Dad. He had his hands jammed into his pockets. Mom was facing him, but he was facing the room, and kept sort of surveying it like he was nervous. His glasses flashed as he turned his head. I'd forgotten he isn't any taller than Mom. She even

157

smiled sometimes as he talked, cocking his head sideways toward her. Then he turned and said something to Janey, and it looked like everyone was smiling.

"You okay?" April asked.

"Yeah," I said, which was the truth. I'd been kind of hunting around inside me for my anger, but I couldn't find it. I kept on bumping into this glad feeling instead, like I was just proud Dad would see the lightning chamber.

I watched Boomer and his bowling buddy, Walter, run up to Dad and then sort of stand there, all awkward, until Walter and Dad shook hands and both boys ran off again.

"He looks different," April said, but of course she hadn't seen Dad since third grade. "Maybe he *is* different. Maybe he's changed."

She sounded all hopeful, as if Dad would make gourmet cheesecake now, and help me with my homework. As if any minute now, he'd come running right over and give me a big, huge hug.

"Forget it, April," I said. "That's *my* dad, not yours."

April didn't look at me. "But he's not George G., either," she said.

I sighed. "Yeah, I know."

"And Philura, here, will show you the lightning chamber," Danny interrupted. An old couple was standing there, looking expectantly at me.

"See ya," I said to April, and showed the grandparents where to put their shoes.

I kept an eye out for Dad, but the crowd seemed to bunch up in front of me, and we got busy again. Then, in a lull, I looked up and Dad was standing there.

He still had his hands in his pockets. He smiled.

"Hi, Curly Top." Like there'd never even *been* any lightning.

"Hi," I said.

He picked up a balloon. "So tell me all about it!"

I took him through the whole routine—with Danny adding comments, of course.

"And Danny, here, will show you the lightning chamber," I said.

Dad stuck out his hand. "Danny Stapleton, I presume? Hi, I'm Mr. Mason."

"Oh, yeah," I said. "Danny, this is my dad." They shook hands.

"Now, sir," Danny said, all high-and-mighty, "prepare yourself for a shock!"

While Dad followed Danny's instructions—took off his shoes and shuffled around on the carpet samples—I started cleaning up rice puffs from the floor. The gym was emptying out. People were heading for the awards ceremony in the auditorium. I heard a tiny zap, and a little chuckle from Dad.

"Great job, you two!" he said, coming into the light again.

"You staying to see us win?" Danny asked.

Dad bent over to tie his shoes. "Wish I could. Gotta get back."

Anger twitched inside me. Dad stood up and stretched.

He smiled at me and started to reach out to ruffle my hair, but his hand hesitated in midair, then passed over his own bald head. I almost felt sad for a second, but when Dad added, "It's a long drive," the anger leaped back so strong I turned away.

He's not George G., I told myself, but I guess I realized right then that being mad at Dad is something I'll just have to live with. At least it'll be easier than living with hives.

"If we win," I said, "I'll show you the ribbon."

"That is, of course," Danny added, hardly grinning at all, "*if* I let her borrow it."

Dad didn't quite look at me. "You could bring it next time you come," he said, as if we didn't both know the third weekend in May was exactly two days away.

"Sure," I said. "I'll bring it Friday—if we win."

I didn't realize how stiff Dad had been till he suddenly relaxed, like he was leaning back in his E-Z Boy.

"You know," he said, "there's a great science museum in Boston."

It sounded like a promise, and I looked at Dad to accept it.

"Wow, yeah!" Danny was chiming in. "My mom keeps saying we ought to go there!"

Dad reached out and ruffled my hair. "Great," he said, only to me. "See you Friday."

I watched Dad stride off across the gym just the way he strides through the bus station.

Danny was watching, too.

"I didn't even know you *had* a dad," he said.

"Yeah. But I guess I do."

Danny was impatient. "Come on. Let's get to the auditorium." But as we walked away from our booth, he stopped for a second to puff up and add, "And how could you say that?—*if* we win! Of course we're going to win, Philura!"